The Australian Citizen

This edition published 2026
by Living Book Press
Copyright © Living Book Press, 2026

ISBN: 978-1-76153-971-8 (hardcover)
         978-1-76153-928-2 (softcover)

First published in 1912.

A catalogue record for this book is available from the National Library of Australia

The Australian Citizen

by

Walter Murdoch, M.A.

CONSIDER WHAT NATION IT IS
WHEREOF YE ARE AND WHEREOF
YE ARE THE GOVERNOURS.
— King James I, *Basilikon Doron* (1599)

A Note from the Publisher

This edition reproduces Walter Murdoch's *The Australian Citizen* (1912) in its original form. Readers will encounter language and ideas that reflect the assumptions, attitudes, and social theories of the early twentieth century. These include outdated racial terminology such as "savages" and "primitive peoples"; colonial viewpoints and harsh judgements about non-European cultures; and extended discussions of the "White Australia" policy—an idea widely taught at the time but one that no longer represents the values of modern Australia or of Living Book Press.

The book also describes social conditions—such as child labour, industrial exploitation, and the lack of legal protections for the vulnerable—that, while disturbing today, were part of the realities Murdoch sought to explain to young Australians of his era.

These elements have been preserved for historical accuracy. Presenting the text exactly as it was written helps readers understand what earlier generations were taught, how those ideas shaped society, and why many of them must now be firmly rejected. Reading such material invites reflection: it reminds us how far Australia has come, and how far we still have to go, in building a society that is genuinely equal, just, and free for all.

Contents

PREFACE.

In order that the reader may not be more disappointed than is necessary, I think it right to explain that this little book was written, primarily, for use in schools; and that I have, throughout, assumed the co-operation of the intelligent teacher. The opening and the concluding portions of the book, especially, will, unless this is borne in mind, be criticised as too abstract and indefinite. Considerations of space have often compelled me to content myself with a broad generalization, leaving it to the teacher to look round—or, better still, to induce his pupils to look round—for concrete examples.

It is hoped that this school-book may possibly appeal to some who, though no longer at school, feel themselves to be beginners in the study of political science.

The book would have been more inadequate than it is, but for the valuable aid ungrudgingly given to the author by Mr. Frank Tate, I.S.O., and Mr. R. R. Garran, C.M.G., to both of whom I desire to express my gratitude. My indebtedness to the *Commonwealth Year Book*—which is one of the very best year books in the world—will be obvious to all readers.

For the benefit of those teachers who may wish to pursue the subject, I append a list of the shorter and more generally accessible of the books which I have myself found useful.

MacCunn.—*Ethics of Citizenship.*
Ritchie, D. G.—*Studies in Social and Political Ethics.*
Marriott.—*English Political Institutions.*
Seeley.—*Introduction to Political Science.*
Bryce.—*Hindrances to Good Citizenship.*
Low.—*The Governance of England.*
Harrison Moore.—*The Commonwealth of Australia.*
Maitland.—*Justice and Police.*

I should like to add that criticisms and suggestions from teachers will be received gratefully and considered attentively.

W. M

Melbourne. *March, 1912*

HOUSE OF PARLIAMENT OF THE COMMONWEALTH

INTRODUCTORY

I.

LINKS

HUMAN beings are bound to one another by various links, which we call relationships. It would not be possible to make a complete list of these relationships, because there are too many of them. The relationship of parent and child, of husband and wife, of master and servant, of king and subject, of officer and private soldier, of employer and employee, of buyer and seller—these are but a few of the most important links which bind people to one another. The more civilized a nation is, the greater the number of links by which members of that nation are connected. The link, for example, which connects you and me at the present moment—the relationship of reader and writer—is one only known to peoples more or less civilized. But no people is so uncivilized that its members are not linked together in a number of ways. Now when we want to speak of human beings, not as separate individuals, but as connected with one another by links or relationships, we use the word "Society."

If you could take to yourself the wings of the morning and fly into the uttermost parts of the earth, wherever you found human beings you would find them *associating* with each other—living together and working together. If you take the wings of history and travel back to the earliest times of which we have any knowledge, you will find the same thing: people living in groups. Every such group we call a society. And the impulse which drives men to associate, the sense of a need for human companionship and human help, we call the social instinct. It is possible for a man to be separated from all society. There was no society on Robinson Crusoe's Island—until Friday appeared, when a society of two came into existence. But Crusoe was never separated from his own social instinct; and this it was which, more than anything else, made his solitude bitter.

People who live in a civilized country are very apt to forget the vast network of human relationships in which they live. Think for a moment of the number and variety of human beings with whom the clothes you are wearing connect you. Some of your garments are woollen; they link you with drovers, and boundary-riders, and shearers, and wool-brokers, and the men who built a factory, and the men who invented the machinery used in it, and the men who brought from the earth the iron of which that machinery is made, and cloth-merchants and tailors and a multitude of others. If some of your garments are made of cotton, that fact connects you with other parts of the world and with another army of workers. If you have any mother-of-pearl buttons, they link you to yet another army—of sailors and divers and merchants and factory-hands. The next time you sit down to dinner, think for a minute or two of the different kinds of labour, in different quarters of the world, which have gone to the preparation of food for you. You will find that a quite ordinary meal is a lesson in geography. It is also a lesson in human relationships.

Nobody, not even the most selfish of us, can possibly cut himself off from human relationships. Even the most selfish of our pleasures depend on the fact that there are other human beings. Take, for instance, the miser's pleasure in his hoard; when he counts his gold so lovingly, his delight is derived, not simply from the fact that he owns a number of coins, but from the fact that he owns more of them than other people. If he discovered that everyone else in the town had a little more money than he, all his delight would be gone—which shows that it had a reference to other people. A girl who takes pride and pleasure in a pretty hat would be neither proud of it nor pleased with it if every other girl in the school appeared in precisely the same kind of hat. Even the most selfish of our enjoyments depend on the fact that we are social beings.

II.

THE POLITICAL LINK

Being by nature social, then, we naturally form societies. A society is a collection of people linked together by some lasting bond or bonds and pursuing some common purpose or purposes. A society may be small or large, simple or complex. A cricket-club is a society; and the British Empire is a society. We who are members of the British Empire are bound to one another by many and various links.

For instance, there is the link of race: the fact that many of us are members of the same race, are more or less distant kinsmen. You and I, if each of us knew his own family tree, would probably find, without going very far back, that we had a common ancestor. Then there is the link of language; it seems obvious that this must be one of the essential links of any society—the fact that its members are able to tell each other what they think and what they want. Then there is the link of religion, which has so powerful a binding force that at one time it seemed strong enough to bind all the nations of Europe in one great society, which was called Christendom; and to set men of different races and different tongues fighting side by side in the crusades. Again, there is the link of tradition: you and I have a common pride in thinking of Quebec and Plassey and Trafalgar and many another terrible and splendid day; we think of Pym and of Cromwell, of Chatham and of Burke, and rejoice together in the courage, wisdom, and strength of these heroes of our history. Again, our common heritage of custom is a powerful link; each of us has been born into a world of customs—of ways of doing things. You did not invent the custom of shaking hands with a friend or of giving presents on a birthday; you found those customs, and thousands of others, awaiting you; and you accept and obey them without thinking. (If you will examine your life for twenty-four hours, you will be surprised to find how little of it is original and independent, and how much consists of just doing what, among people of British origin, it is customary to do.) And yet again, there is the link of ideas, and especially of moral ideas. You and I find ourselves in a world where certain kinds of conduct are thought to be right, and certain other kinds wrong. Multitudes of men are bound together by the fact that they agree, in the main, as to the way in which it is fitting for a human being to live; that they have pretty much the same way of looking at questions of right and wrong.

But if you look at these links, one by one, you will see that none of them can be *the* link binding together all members of the British Empire; indeed, each of them is more likely to bind us to some people outside the Empire than to certain of our fellow-members. For instance, the link of language binds us to the Americans of the United States, but not to the Dutch of South Africa. The link of race ought to bind us more closely to the inhabitants of Germany than to the French inhabitants of Canada; and so on. What then is the link which connects you and me as members of the British Empire, and which does not connect us with the members of any other society? It is to be found in the word *fellow-subjects*. If we are members of the British Empire, we are subjects of the same sovereign. But the meaning of this is not yet perfectly clear, because, as we shall see presently, the word sovereign may mean a king or queen, or it may mean a chosen body of persons, or it may mean the whole nation. It will be simpler, for the present, to say that we are citizens of the same great State.

But, you may say, surely this is just telling us the same thing twice over; for *society* and *state* mean precisely the same thing. No: they do not mean the same thing. The state is a kind of machinery[1] which a society gradually constructs in order to protect its members from enemies outside and inside the society, and in order to help its members to lead the life which, according to the ideas of that society, is fittest for a human being to lead. In other words, the state is the means by which society tries to help every individual member to realise his highest possibilities—to lead the best life possible to him. The work of the state is to remove from every person's path the obstacles which would prevent him from living this best life; to secure certain essential conditions, without which this best life is for ever impossible to him.

Can we name these essential conditions? We can: their names are Liberty and Justice.

The business of the state, then, is to secure the utmost possible measure of liberty to all its members, and to maintain justice between one member and another. But it is obvious that the very first duty which society owes to its members is to preserve itself from destruction; to guard itself against attacks by an enemy. This duty, also, it performs by means of the machinery which we call the State.

The reason why society does these things for its members is, as you will see if you think for a minute or two, that it can do them infinitely better than its members could, each acting separately.

---

1   If this book had not been intended mainly for youthful readers, I should have made a distinction here. Government would have been spoken of as the machine, the State as society organised to use the machinery of government. But on the whole, I have thought the statement in the text less likely to be misunderstood.

III.

SOCIETY'S MACHINE

Man is sometimes distinguished as the tool-using animal; but some of the lower animals also use tools. Monkeys, for instance, will use stones and sticks as weapons—and weapons are one kind of tools. But man is the tool-*making* animal. The monkey uses a stone or a stick as he finds it lying about; he does not try to change it. It is only a man who will take the stone, grind it to a sharp edge, and lash the stick to it, so as to make an axe. So it is with that tool which we call *government*, or *the state*. Many of the lower animals have a kind of government. A herd of elephants, for instance, has its leader and its sentinels; so has a herd of buffaloes. The bees have a queen, a small class of idlers, and a large class of labourers with various duties allotted to them. But the form of government of an elephant herd does not change from century to century; the bees' commonwealth is the same today as it was when a Roman poet described it two thousand years ago. Human beings, on the other hand, have constantly changed and are constantly changing their form of government. There is a vast difference, is there not? between a primitive weapon, such as the stone axe I have spoken of, and a vast and complicated weapon such as a great modern battleship. Yet that difference is hardly so vast as the difference between the government of a primitive horde or clan and the government of a great modern people. The modern state is the greatest, the most complex, the most wonderful of all the machines that man has devised. When we open our eyes and look at it, we see that this is so; but we very rarely do open our eyes and look at it. We are so accustomed to it that we take it for granted, as we take for granted the air we breathe and many another blessing.

How has this great and complicated machine come to be what it is? You sometimes hear it spoken of as if it had simply grown like a tree, gradually, silently, and without effort of its own. But the state did not grow like a tree into its present form, any more than the stone axe grew like a tree until it became a battleship. It was made into what it is by conscious effort—by the efforts of many generations of men. Changes have continually taken place; parts of the machine that worked badly have been removed, and better parts have been put in their place; ingenious devices have been adopted; a safety-valve has been added here, and there a piston has been lengthened; gradually the machine has been made to do more and more work, and to do it better. But every change has first been an idea in the mind of a thinking man, and has been turned into reality by the painful efforts of men. All the liberty we enjoy, the peace, the safety, the comfort, the well-being which our form of government secures for us—all has been won for us by the efforts of those who went before us, and in some cases by their agony and blood. They fought and died to hand down to us what we accept almost without noticing it. And it is only by our own effort that this machine can be kept running smoothly and doing its work well; it is only by our own effort that it can be improved, so that it may do its work better.

> *It was not made with the mountains; it is not one with the deep.*
> *Men, not gods, devised it. Men, not gods, must keep.*

IV.

FREE WHEELS

Though it may seem desirable to use the word "machinery" in describing the state, we must remember that it is very different from any other machine. It is a machine guided and controlled and driven by its own parts. It is a machine, each of whose parts is made of flesh and blood, and moved by hopes and fears and by various and innumerable desires. Most wonderful of all, it is a machine whose every part has a will of its own, and is free to choose between working well and working badly.

The parts of this great political machine are called citizens. You and I are citizens whether we like it or not. It will not do to say that we prefer to be private individuals, and will leave others to be citizens if they like. "Citizen" is simply the name we give to a human being when we think of the political side of him; you may say that you have no political side, but it would be just as sensible to say that you have no left side. Man is by nature, as a great Greek philosopher said, a political animal: you may determine not to be political, but it would be just as sensible to determine not to be an animal. No; we are wheels in the great machine, whether we like it or not,—but we are free wheels: free to choose between doing our work well and doing it badly. We are citizens, and we cannot help being citizens; all that is left for us to choose is whether we will be good or bad citizens.

The first duty of a citizen is to try to understand the machinery of which he is a part; for it is another curious thing about this extraordinary machine, that it will never work really well until its parts understand what they are doing. In this little book I shall try to give, in the simplest language I can find, an account of the institutions in the midst of which, and by means of which, you and I must play our parts as citizens.

PART I.
GOVERNMENT

CHAPTER I.

WHAT IS GOVERNMENT

If you have ever watched little boys playing marbles in a school playground, you must have noticed that the game was constantly interrupted by short but heated disputes. And if, being something of a philosopher, you have asked yourself why so simple a thing as a game of marbles should cause a succession of little quarrels, you have probably discovered that these quarrels arise from two sources: they are either disputes about the rules of the game, or disputes about whether this or that player has broken the rules. In a cricket or football match there is, as a general thing, no quarrelling; that is because, in the first place, the players know the rules very well, and do not disobey them; and because, in the second place, there is an umpire to *apply the rules* to individual cases. In cricket, for instance, he will say whether this or that batsman is out or not; in football, he will decide whether this or that player has held the ball too long; and so on. No well-conducted player ever thinks of questioning the umpire's authority.

We cannot imagine any game being played without rules, or without obedience to the rules on the part of the players. Now life is a much more complicated thing than any game; and it requires a far greater number of rules. And life offers people severe temptations to break the rules; a strong force is therefore required to prevent the rules from being disobeyed.

It is a fact, unfortunately, that all human relationships give occasion for quarrelling, because all of them give occasion for injustice. If you will look at the examples of relationships which I gave on the first page, you will see that this is so. The parent may treat his child unjustly; the king may treat his subject unjustly; the employer may treat his employee unjustly; the officer may treat the private soldier unjustly; and so with all the rest. And therefore it is necessary to have rules governing all these relationships; otherwise there would be constant quarrelling all round us. And a society in which there is constant quarrelling is in a very bad state; firstly, because there can be no peace or comfort or real liberty for the members of such a society; and, secondly, because a society torn asunder by quarrels cannot present a strong, united front to an enemy,—it will fall before the next foe that comes against it. That, then, is the first reason why *government* is necessary: that *order* may be maintained,—order, which protects a society against attacks from outside, and which is necessary to the well-being of every member of the society. To maintain order, *rules* are necessary; and so government means, for one thing, the making of rules—or *laws*. The making of laws we call "legislation."

But rules are of no use unless they are obeyed. In cricket there is an umpire, to apply the rules; and in the larger life of society we need an umpire constantly. When two people quarrel, who is going to say which is in the right? When a man is accused of having broken the law, who is going to say whether he has really broken the law? And, if he has, who is going to decide what punishment he deserves? This, also, is a part of government: to apply the laws to particular cases; to judge between man and man, and to judge between men and the laws. Government does this by means of its law-courts, which will be described later on.

Then, obviously, when the judges say that a man has broken a certain law and deserves a certain punishment, he must be punished; and who is to punish him? This, again, is one of the duties of government; it is a part of the public work which government must perform. If it did not punish people for breaking the laws, it might as well not make laws at all.

But government must do a great deal of other public works besides punishing. This brings us to another reason, besides the maintaining of order, why government is necessary. There are many things which a society as a whole can do, which could not be done nearly so well, if they could be done at all, by private members of society acting separately. Take, for instance, the work of keeping the society ready, in time of peace, for an attack by an enemy; or the work of conducting a war. It is vitally necessary to every one of us that Australia should be properly defended; but no one of us, acting separately and as a private individual, could do anything to keep an enemy out of Australia. This is what we call *public work*: society, as a whole, must do this work; and it does it by means of government. Or, in other words, the State does it. Another example of public work is the carrying of letters all over the country; another is the education of the young. It is true that government often does work which private individuals *could* manage to do; for instance, the railways, which in Australia are thought of as public work, and managed by the government, are in other countries (Britain for example) managed by private individuals, who form themselves into little companies for the purpose. But this only means that the managing of railways is not *necessarily* public work; it is not a *necessary part* of the work of government. But defence, and the punishment of offenders against the law, are necessarily public work, and could not be done except by the State.

Now I must ask you to remember three long words. We have seen that government consists of three different kinds of work: the making of laws, the applying of the laws to particular cases, and the doing of public work. And these three tasks require three different bodies of men to carry them out. The body which makes the laws is called the *legislature*. The body which applies the laws to particular cases is called the *judiciary*. And the body which does the public work is called the *executive*. (Only, as a matter of fact, certain members of the executive may be—and in Australia, and in Britain, always are—members of the legislature too.) These three—legislature, judiciary, executive,—may be called the three *organs of government*.

At this point you will be inclined to say—It seems, then, that government must be the great enemy to liberty; for government means, among other things, making laws, and insisting on our obedience to the laws; and laws are simply restraints on liberty. Liberty, you will say, means being able to do exactly as we please; and a law is just a way of stopping people from doing exactly as they please. So that government seems to be another name for interference with our personal liberty.

If so, savages must have much more liberty than we have, who are members of a civilized society. For in a civilized society, as we have seen, relationships are far more numerous and complicated than amongst savages; and so the government of a civilized society is a far greater and more complicated thing than the government of a savage tribe. But if you have ever read anything about the ways of a savage tribe, you know that the savage, far from having more liberty than you have, has infinitely less: he is, compared with you, an absolute slave. He is a slave to his chief; and he is a slave to the customs of his tribe. Indeed, if I had space for it... I could show you that the very idea of personal liberty does not occur to a primitive people; it only enters into men's minds when they are more or less civilized. So that government does not seem, after all, to be the enemy of liberty; it seems to be actually the best friend liberty has. In a later chapter, after we have looked a little at the machinery of government, I shall try to show you that this is really so. I shall consider the question, what liberty means; and I shall show you that it does not mean mere freedom from restraint, but something much better worth having. And I shall try to convince you, that, whatever may be said of bad government, good government is the truest friend of true liberty.

CHAPTER II.

DIFFERENT KINDS OF GOVERNMENT.

The ancient Greeks were the first people who thought hard about the question, *what is the best kind of government?* and it was a Greek thinker who first tried to classify political constitutions,—that is, to make a list of the different ways in which people may be governed; for the *constitution* of a country just means the way in which that country is governed. He saw that the nature of a constitution depends on whether the sovereignty—the supreme and absolute power, from which there is no appeal—belongs to one person, or to a few, or to the many. Using words which we have borrowed from the Greeks, if the sovereignty belongs to one person, we may call that constitution a *monarchy*; if to a few, we may call it an *oligarchy*; if to the many, we may call it a *democracy*.

But this classification will not do for us at the present time; as you can see if you can imagine that ancient Greek thinker coming to life again today in Australia. For, first, he would hear men talking about the King, and would of course conclude that he was living in a monarchy. Then he would go to Parliament House and see a few men engaged in making laws for the whole country, and he would say—why, this is not a monarchy, but an oligarchy. And then he would be told that if those men in Parliament tried to govern in opposition to the wishes of the majority of the nation—of *the many*, as he would say,—they would be sent away and not allowed to govern any more; and he would conclude that, after all, it was neither a monarchy nor an oligarchy, but a democracy. And then it would be time for someone to explain to him, that a new kind of government had been invented since his time, a kind of government which neither he nor any other of the ancient Greeks ever thought of: and that it was called *representative* GOVERNMENT.

When we read of that wonderful people, the Greeks, and of their great services to civilization,—when we read of their great poets and historians, sculptors and architects, thinkers and teachers, law-givers and statesmen and generals,—we are inclined to think that Greece must have been a very great state indeed. But it was not a great state; it was not a state at all. Athens was a state; Sparta was a state; but Greece as a whole was not a state; it had no common government. Greece to us seems a very small country, but to the ancient Greeks it seemed far too large a country to be a single state. To them, the city was the state, and the state was the city. If we could show one of them a map of New South Wales, and tell him the number of its inhabitants, and say *"That is a state,"* he would say—*"How can that be? How can you possibly get all those people to travel all those miles to Sydney, in order that they may decide about the making of a new law?"* Among the Greeks, you see, the state *had* to be small; every citizen took his share in the work of governing, and therefore had to be within easy reach of the place where the governing assembly met. The citizen did his public duty in his own person, not, as we do, by entrusting the work to *representatives.*

Of course it would be quite impossible for Australia to be governed like that. It would be quite impossible to get all the grown-up people to leave their homes and to come from the most distant parts of this vast continent to some central place of meeting, every time a new law had to be made. And even if we could get them to come, where could we put them? What building would hold so enormous a multitude? And how would the business of governing be done by a meeting of two million people, when a meeting of a thousand people is far too large to get any real business done?

As you probably know, if you have read your history, we have got over this difficulty by the device of representative government; that is, by entrusting the actual work of government to a few men who *represent* those who have chosen them. And as these chosen men are responsible to those who chose them for the way in which they govern, this kind of government is also called *responsible government*. The men thus chosen form the *governing body*. You are not to suppose, however, that we in Australia are governed by one governing body and no other. There are in Australia a great number of governing bodies, as we shall see. And we shall also see that every Australian citizen has something to do with at least four different governing bodies.

CHAPTER III.

LOCAL GOVERNMENT.

The first *"governing body"* which I am going to ask you to think about is the body which carries on the work of *local government*; that is, the body which governs the town or district or *locality* in which you live. I take this kind of government first, both because it is the simplest and most easily explained, and also because the results of it are the most easily seen and understood; you cannot step through your garden-gate into the street without seeing one, at least, of the things that local government does for you. Afterwards I shall go on to speak of State government, of Federal government, and of Imperial government. Each of these kinds of government is carried on by its own governing body; these are the four governing bodies of which I spoke in the last chapter.

(Hitherto I have been using the word *"state"* in the sense of the whole machinery of government; henceforth I shall use it in its narrower sense, as meaning one of the six great divisions of Australia.)

"But," you will say, *"if no fewer than four different bodies of men are engaged in governing me, I am a very much governed person! And how am I going to obey all these bodies? What shall I do when their orders clash? Which must I obey?"* The answer is, that their orders do not clash. They deal with entirely different matters. The Imperial governing body, sitting at Westminster, deals with matters which concern the Empire as a whole. The Federal governing body deals with matters which concern Australia as a whole. The State govern-

ing body deals with whatever concerns the particular state, in which you happen to live, as a whole. And the local governing body deals only with those matters which concern one small division of the state, the particular locality in which you live.

I have spoken of government as a thing which has been gradually fashioned by human effort, and have warned you against thinking of it as a thing which grew like a tree. And yet at this point a tree is the very best image I can find to illustrate the relation of these different governing bodies to one another. The trunk of the tree is the Imperial governing body or Parliament; the great branches which spring from that trunk are the parliaments of the great dominions of the Empire—Australia, Canada, South Africa, and New Zealand. (I do not mention India, because India is not a self-governing part of the Empire.) The smaller branches which spring from each of these great limbs are the parliaments of the states into which each of the dominions is divided; and the twigs are the little parliaments, or *councils* as they are generally called, which govern the towns and districts within each state.

Now of course we may say that a twig is not a very important part of a tree; you might cut off a twig, or even a whole bundle of twigs, without much altering the general appearance of the tree; you might even prune away *all* the twigs, and a great and strong tree would still remain. In the same way your shire council, or town council, may be called an unimportant body; it deals only with what concerns your own little corner of the state, and therefore you may say that its work is limited to a few tasks, and those very simple. But a tree without twigs would not be a very comfortable place for birds to live in and build their nests in; and you would find life very much less comfortable than it is, if the local governing bodies were done away with. Their work is really a very important part of government, and it cannot be properly carried on by foolish or idle persons. We ought therefore to be very careful in choosing persons who are to represent us in these councils.

Though the manner in which local government is carried on is not precisely the same in all the Australian states, the differences are not now very important; and the following description of the machinery, and the work it does, may be taken as applying to all the states.

For the purposes of local government, the whole state is mapped out into *municipalities*[2]. A municipality may be a large district, with not very many people to the square mile, in which case it is called a *shire*; or it may be a small, thickly-peopled district, in which case it is called a *borough*, or a *town*, or a *city*. The municipality, of whatever kind it be, is divided into parts; and the inhabitants of each part, on a fixed day, choose a representative—someone whom they think fit to do the work of governing the municipality. The men thus chosen by the various parts form the municipal *council*—shire council, borough council, town council, or city council, as the case may be. And this council meets, in a building which belongs to the municipality, and carries on the work which the Parliament of the state has set apart for such councils to carry on.

For you must not suppose that a municipal council can do anything it likes, or anything it considers necessary to the welfare of the municipality. Its powers are strictly limited; they have been fixed by the law of the land. It is *required* to deal with certain matters, and *allowed* to deal with certain other matters; beyond these it is not allowed to go. The most important matters with which it may deal are—roads and streets; lighting; traffic; drainage; public health; bridges, ferries, wharves, and jetties; fire-brigades; public recreation-grounds; hospitals; and markets. It also has something to say in the

---

2   The Latin word *municipium* meant a town outside of Rome; a town whose inhabitants were Roman citizens, but which was nevertheless a free town, governed by its own laws; i.e., a town which enjoyed the benefits of local government.

A FIRE BRIGADE MOTOR.

erection of all new buildings, and the repair or destruction of old ones which have become dangerous.

As a matter of fact, however, some of these duties are in many cases not carried out by a municipal council but by another body— a board, or trust, as it is often called. One instance may be given: the drainage and water-supply of Melbourne. Melbourne is not a municipality, but a cluster of municipalities—shires and towns and cities. Now the drainage and water-supply of these are matters which could perhaps be managed by each municipality separately, but which can be much better managed by one body which does the work for all the municipalities. These two pieces of work have therefore been handed over to a body called The Melbourne and Metropolitan Board of Works, whose members are chosen by the various municipal councils. Similarly there are, in the various states, Boards of Health, Fire Brigades Boards, Harbour Trusts, Road Boards, and so forth. But all of them are parts of the machinery of local government; they all do the kind of work that we have in mind when we speak of local government.

Undoubtedly one of the chief tasks of a municipal council is the making, and keeping-up, of roads; and if you think local government an unimportant matter, that must be because you are so accustomed to the use of roads, and good roads, that you never stop and think what it would be like to live in a country where there were no roads. Why, civilization itself would have been impossible without roads, which allow people to visit each other and exchange ideas; such intercourse is the mother of civilization. And roads allow us to exchange not only ideas, but goods; the exchange of goods is called trade, and trade has been one of the great civilizers of mankind. You can almost tell what state of civilization a country has reached, by the number and quality of the roads in that country. Here then is an example of the way in which government increases the comfort of every member of society; and not his comfort only, but his liberty too; for roads enable us to travel, set us free to move about the country in a way which would be impossible without them. We need not be surprised to find that, in the state in which we live, many millions of pounds have been spent on making roads and keeping them in repair. Take, again, the lighting of the streets, and the fact that we can walk about the brightly-lighted streets of a modern city as safely by night as by day. To understand what a blessing this is, one has to read a description of some European town a few hundred years ago, when respectable people dared not walk abroad after nightfall for fear of thieves and murderers. Or, again, take the water supply; do those who live in large cities always remember what "government" means to them, even in this one matter? The next time you turn on the tap in your bath-room, think for a moment of the enormous reservoir, of the great channels, of the intricate network of pipes, of the army of men who have set all this working, of the army who are employed every day in keeping up this vast system which enables us to use pure water almost as freely and as unthinkingly as we use the air. Or take, finally, public health. What! you will say; does the shire council keep me from falling sick, or cure me when I am sick? No, it cannot quite do that; the best shire council in the world has not done away with the need for doctors; still less has it done away with the need for taking care of our own bodies. But local government does a great many things to help us to keep healthy,—things that we could not possibly do for ourselves. By looking after the drainage and the water-supply, for instance, and by many other means, it prevents diseases of various kinds from taking hold of a town. It prevents foolish or dirty people from doing things which are dangerous to the health of others; and when an infectious disease does break out, it prevents that disease from spreading. To appreciate this blessing properly, you must live for a short time, or at least imagine yourself living, in one of those great foul cities of the East, where, as we read in our newspapers from time to time, an epidemic breaks out and spreads with fearful rapidity and carries off hundreds of thousands.

But in order to perform its various tasks, of course the municipal council needs money; where is that money to come from? Naturally, it must come from the people for whose benefit the work is done. Those who own or occupy houses within the municipality, or who own land in it, have to pay their share towards the expenses of governing the municipality; a small or a large share, according as the value of their property is small or large. The sum they pay is called the municipal rate; and the persons who pay these rates—the *ratepayers*—are the only persons allowed to have a voice in the choosing of men to carry on the work of local government.

Payment of these rates is compulsory: we are compelled to pay them; it is not left to our own free choice whether we shall pay them or not. If it were so left,—if the council were merely allowed to ask us politely for a certain sum of money, without the power to enforce its demand,—it is to be feared that the council would not be able to make very many roads or build very good bridges. Some of us, I am afraid, would argue that the council did not need so much money; some would say that they did not want so many roads and bridges, and therefore should not be asked to pay for them; some would easily persuade themselves that they were really too poor to pay so much; and some, without arguing against the rates, would nevertheless forget to pay them. So the money would not come in; the public work could not be done; and the public would suffer for lack of it. It is necessary, therefore, that the council should be able, if need be, to compel us to pay the rates. It is necessary, too,—for the same reasons,—that the council should be able to compel us to accept the rules it makes and obey the orders it gives,—so long, of course, as it deals only with those matters in which it has been given authority over us.

Here, then, in this very simplest of all forms of government, we find four features which we shall find in all the other forms of government of which in this book I shall have to speak.

(1) Government implies *compulsion*; unless the governing body can compel obedience on the part of the governed, there can be no such thing as real government.

(2) Government implies taxation; the work of governing costs money, and must be paid for by the governed.

(3) Government—as we in Australia know it—is carried on in the interests, not of the governing body, but of the people who are governed. Roads, for instance, are not made for the benefit of the members of the council, but for the benefit of the whole municipality.

(4) Government, among us, is carried on by a body of men chosen by the governed. This, as we have already seen, is what is meant by "representative government"; it may also be called *self-government*, for when we are governed by men chosen by ourselves from among ourselves, we may really be said to govern ourselves.

CHAPTER IV.

THE GOVERNMENT OF THE STATE.

Just as the members of a cricket-club meet and choose certain of their own number to form a committee and manage the affairs of the club, so the members of a municipality choose certain of their own number to form a council and manage the affairs of the municipality. In exactly the same way, the members of a state choose certain of their own number to form a Parliament and manage the affairs of the state as a whole. If you are a member of a municipality, you must also be a member of the state of which that municipality is a part; so that it comes to this,—as member of a municipality, you help to choose a member of the municipal council; as member of a state, you help to choose a member of the state Parliament.

I have tried to show you that the matters with which local government deals are far from being trifling or unimportant matters; on the contrary, some of them are matters which vitally affect our comfort and general well-being. But, for all that, the local governing body is not nearly so important a body as the state Parliament, for several reasons.

(1) The local governing body deals only with matters which affect one small corner of the state, while the Parliament deals with matters which affect the state as a whole. If a town council does its work badly, the result will be felt throughout the town; but if the Parliament does its work badly, the result will be felt from one end of the state to the other. (2) The things which are done by the local

governing body, though they may be important, are few in number; whereas the Parliament of the state deals with an enormous number and a vast variety of things. (3) The local governing body has no powers of its own; all the powers it exercises are such as the Parliament has chosen to entrust to it; and the Parliament which gave these powers may take them away again if it chooses. If the Parliament, for instance, should come to the conclusion that it could manage the business of road-making better than the municipal councils can, it could forbid the municipal councils to have anything to do with road-making for the future, and the councils would have to obey.

But why, you may ask, do we have these local governing bodies? Could not the state Parliament do the work? Undoubtedly it could; but I think there are three chief reasons why it does not attempt to do so. (1) If the state Parliament had to look after every matter of public importance in every shire and town in the state, as well as the matters which concern the state as a whole, it could not possibly find time to do its work well. (2) People on the spot know what is needed for their own locality far better than people at a distance do. If a street in a distant country town could not be mended until a body of men, meeting in a city scores or perhaps hundreds of miles away, could be persuaded that it really needed mending, the work might be put off for a long time, and might not be so well done in the end. (3) It is good that as many of us as possible should learn by experience what the business of governing actually means. It is good for a man's character, that he should have responsibility on his shoulders. Local government provides a *political training* for thousands of citizens. We may add (4) that local government tends to check extravagance. People who want a piece of work done are not so apt to be wasteful if they have to pay for the whole of it themselves.

Turning, then, from local government to the government of the state as a whole, we find that this latter work, in Australia, is carried on by a Parliament, which is closely modelled on the British Parliament. I need not here tell you—for you have read elsewhere—of the centuries of effort, experiment, and strife through which Britain sought for the perfect machinery of self-government; how she gradually fashioned for herself a machine which, though far from perfect, was at least good enough to be imitated by every civilized nation; how the people strove to make their Parliament supreme, so that the will of the King himself should not prevail against it; and how, having won that victory, they had to strive to make their Parliament really represent them. All this work, or nearly all of it, was already done by the time the Australian States were fit for Parliaments of their own; so that, in modelling our Parliament on that of Britain, we shared in the result of centuries of effort on the part of patriotic Britons.

But we ought to remember that Britain gave us something more than a model, to imitate if we could. If you know your Australian history, you will remember that when the first settlement was made, that small society was governed by one man, Governor Phillip, who was empowered "to make ordinances for the good government of the settlement"; that is, he was practically an absolute monarch, and no one else had any share in the responsibility of governing. It is true that he was responsible to the British Parliament for the way in which he governed the colony; but so far as the other colonists were concerned, whatever orders he chose to give had the force of law. It was not till 1823 that the British Parliament established a small council to advise the Governor in making and carrying out the laws; but this council was not chosen by the people, so that it did not bring us much nearer to self-government. In 1842 a real Parliament was given to New South Wales, with two-thirds of its members elected by the inhabitants of the colony; but even this was not self-government, for the executive part of government— the carrying out of the laws—was still left to the Governor and to men chosen by him; and there can be no real self-government so long as the executive is not controlled by the people, as we shall see

BURRINJUCK IRRIGATION WORKS, N.S.W.

later on. It was not until 1850 that the British Parliament passed an "Australian Colonies Government Act," which gave real self-government to the earliest Australian states. Queensland became a separate self-governing state in 1859; Western Australia, latest of all, did not obtain self-government until 1890. In each case, the freedom to govern itself and manage its own affairs was granted to the Australian state by an Act of the British Parliament.

Australians ought always to remember—what they are very apt to forget—that self-government, with its splendid privileges and its heavy responsibilities, was a present to the Australian states from the people of Britain. We ought to remember, also, that this present would have been a bitter mockery if Britain had not given us another present as well—her protection. Britain said to us, "You can make your own laws and manage your own affairs, and I shall not interfere with you;" but she added—"and I shall see that no other nation interferes with you." We ought always to remember that, if we have been governing ourselves all these years, we have been doing so under the shadow of the Union Jack. But for that protection, some other nation would, in all probability, have long ago taken possession of Australia.

The constitution of an Australian state, then, is modelled on the British constitution. (Remember that "constitution" just means the *form* of government, the way in which the work of government is carried on.) By the British constitution, the *legislative sovereignty*—the supreme law-making power, from which there can be no appeal to any higher authority, because there is no higher human authority—rests with Parliament; and Parliament consists of three parts: King, Lords, and Commons. So, in an Australian state, the sovereignty rests with the King and with two Houses of Parliament—the Legislative Council, generally called the Upper House, and the Legislative Assembly, generally called the Lower House. And in many other ways, down to minute details, our state constitution is modelled on the British. We must notice, however, three important differences.

(1) Just as we choose men to be our representatives in the state Parliament, so also a man is chosen to represent the King, who cannot come himself. The King's representative is called the Governor of the state, and he forms an important link between an Australian state and the Parliament of Great Britain. (2) The sovereignty of the British Parliament is *absolute*; it can make laws about anything, and can even alter the constitution itself. Whereas the Australian state parliaments are only sovereign in *some matters*; there are many things, as we shall see, about which they cannot make laws. (3) With us[3], the Upper House, as well as the Lower, is chosen by the people; whereas the British House of Lords, as you know, is not chosen by the British people; so that our Parliaments are more thoroughly *representative* of the people than the British Parliament.

What, then, are the matters with which state government deals? What does the state Parliament actually do? Some of the more important things it does will be described in later chapters; here I shall only repeat, that state government is concerned with those matters which affect the state as a whole, and which could not safely be left to the different municipalities to manage for themselves. For instance: it is felt to be essential to the welfare of the state as a whole, that every citizen of the state should have at least a school education; the state governing body therefore makes laws about education, and sees that they are carried out in every corner of the state. Again, the great system of railways, by which we, and our goods, are carried from one end of the state to the other,—the good management of this system is a thing that affects, not this or that municipality, but the state as a whole; this, therefore, is a matter which (in Australia) state government deals with. Again, if a disease breaks out among

3   This is not true of New South Wales or Queensland.

the apple-trees, unless it is stamped out, it will quickly spread to the orchards of the whole state; the state governing body must take measures to stamp it out. The municipal councils may, as we have seen, do much for the health of their own districts; but there are some matters affecting the health of the whole state—such, for instance, as the sale of impure foods under false pretences—which can be dealt with only by the state Parliament. In a thousand ways, small and great, the governing body of the state seeks to preserve and to increase the welfare of the whole state. It helps the poor, the sick, and the aged; it tries to maintain justice—to see that every citizen is fairly and justly treated by his fellow-citizens; it does its best to prevent crime, and punishes those who break the laws; and it collects money from the citizens—in the form of *taxes*—to pay for all this public work.

CHAPTER V.

STATES AND COMMONWEALTH.

The municipal council, as we have seen, does things which affect the whole municipality, things which private individuals could not do at all, or could not do so well. The state Parliament, in like manner, does things which affect the whole state, things which neither private individuals, nor municipal councils, could do for themselves. But there are some things which affect the whole of Australia; and it was long ago felt that a central governing body for the whole of Australia could do these things much better than they could be done by the states acting separately. What these things are, we shall see presently.

So early as 1847 an English statesman, Earl Grey, wrote his opinion that there *were* some matters affecting Australia as a whole, "the regulation of which, in some uniform manner and by some single authority, may be essential to the welfare of them all"; i.e. to the welfare of all the separate states, or colonies, as they were then called. But at that moment Australians were thinking more about the need of splitting-up than about the need of uniting; the people of Port Phillip—now Victoria—were striving to be allowed to separate from New South Wales; and when Port Phillip had its way, the Moreton Bay District—now Queensland—began to call out for separation too. (Tasmania had been a separate colony since 1823.) Earl Grey's words were taken no notice of because at the time when they were spoken, Australians were becoming more and more certain that Australia could not be well governed by a single authority; that the various parts of it required separate governing bodies of their own. And so Australia was split up into six different states. And yet, as time passed, people came more and more to think that Earl Grey was right, and that there were matters about which it would be better for some central authority to decide. Thus, only seventeen years after the separation of Victoria from New South Wales, we find Sir Henry Parkes declaring that "the time has arrived when these colonies should be united by some federal bond." And from that time onward, the need of such a federal bond was ever more keenly felt; it was talked about in private and in public; the newspapers discussed it; books were written about it; thoughtful and patriotic men in all the states argued about the best way of bringing it into existence; and at last meetings were held, to which each of the states sent representatives, to devise a constitution for the whole of Australia. The constitution so framed was passed into law by the British Parliament; and, finally, on September 17th, 1900, Queen Victoria signed a proclamation declaring that "on and after the first day of January, 1901, the people of New South Wales, Victoria, South Australia, Queensland, Tasmania, and Western Australia shall be united in a Federal Commonwealth, under the name of the Commonwealth of Australia." So our Commonwealth came into existence on the first day of the twentieth century.

Now it is important that we should understand exactly what is meant by this "federal bond" which binds together the six states of Australia; for there may be all sorts of bonds between states or nations, some very loose and elastic, some very tight and rigid. One kind of bond is called an alliance. When, for example, in 1902, Great Britain entered into an alliance with Japan, the bond simply meant a general agreement between the two nations to help each other wherever possible; and they even agreed that either of them would, if certain circumstances arose, take up arms in defence of the other. Neither nation gave up one jot of its power to the other by this alliance. But when in 1800 Ireland formed a Union with Great Britain, it was a very different kind of bond that came into existence; for Ireland did give up power,—she gave up her Parliament; and thenceforward neither England, nor Scotland, nor Ireland, nor Wales, had a parliament of its own: the supreme power rested with the parliament of the United Kingdom sitting at Westminster. Now the federal bond is neither an alliance, like the Anglo-Japanese alliance, in which both the allied nations retain all their powers; nor is it a complete union, like the union of Great Britain and Ireland, where the full sovereignty rests with the one central government. The federal bond means that a number of separate governments hand over *a part* of their sovereignty—hand over their right to govern, *so far as certain matters are concerned*,—to a central authority (called the federal government), but retain the rest of their sovereignty.

It will make this clearer if I point out that the relation between the municipal councils and the state parliament is a very different thing from the relation between the state parliament and the federal parliament. For the municipal council has no powers of its own; such powers as it exercises are entrusted to it by the state parliament. But the state parliament has powers of its own, which the Commonwealth parliament cannot touch. Just as I am bound to obey the orders of the ship's captain so long as I am on board his ship, but when I step ashore his authority over me ceases, so we are bound to obey the state government in its own sphere, but outside of that sphere it has no authority whatever. And in like manner the federal government is supreme only in its own sphere. The Constitution of the Australian Commonwealth tells us what the two spheres are; it tells us with what matters federal government deals, what duties federal government has taken over from state government.

The Australian Commonwealth was not the first, but the fifth, great modern federation. In linking themselves together in this way, the Australian states were but following the example set by the states of the American Union, by the cantons of Switzerland, by the king-doms and duchies of Germany, and by the provinces of Canada. In each of these cases, it was war, or the danger of war, that impelled the different states to unite. In the case of the Australian states, no doubt the thought of how helpless they would be, if they remained disunited, to defend themselves against foreign invasion, had some-thing to do with their union; but probably their strongest motive was the sense of nationhood,—the feeling that we Australians are one nation; that the welfare of every part of Australia is bound up with the welfare of every other part; that therefore we ought not to quarrel with one another, and that we ought to remove all possible causes of quarrelling with one another. And there is no doubt that having a central government for the whole continent has greatly strengthened and deepened this sense of national *oneness*.

CHAPTER VI.

THE COMMONWEALTH.

As we have seen, the *Constitution* of a country is just a name for *the way in which that country is governed*; and, as we have also seen, one great difference between constitutions is a matter of the sovereignty; some placing the sovereign power in the hands of one man or woman, some in the hands of a few, some in the hands of the whole people. But there are many other differences, and one is the difference between *written* and *unwritten* constitutions. The British Constitution, though many important parts of it are written in the laws of the land,—as, for instance, in the great Habeas Corpus Act about which you have read,—may, on the whole, be described as an "unwritten" constitution. A great deal of it is made up of old customs which have never been turned into written laws. But the constitution of the Australian Commonwealth, like that of the United States of America, is a written one; it has been printed in full, and we can all get hold of a copy of it without much trouble. (It is printed, for instance, in the first *Commonwealth Year-Book*, a copy of which is, or ought to be, in every school library in Australia.)

If you think for a moment you will see why it was very important that the Commonwealth constitution should be written down clearly in black and white. The federation of Australia meant this: that the Australian people decided that, for the good of the whole of Australia, the separate states ought to surrender certain of their governing powers to a central authority; this central authority to be appointed by the whole people. It meant that, in certain matters—and in those matters only—they preferred to be governed by one central parliament rather than by the parliaments of the separate states. They did not for a moment intend to be governed by this central parliament in *all* matters with which government deals, but only in a few. It was very necessary to have a written document clearly setting forth what these matters were; otherwise there would be constant disputing as to whether this thing or that thing should be dealt with by the state governments or by the Commonwealth government. In other words, the states were giving away certain of their powers; it was necessary for them to know exactly what these powers were, and to have the bargain clearly written down so that there might be no mistake in the future as to what they had intended.

Perhaps I can make this clearer by pointing out a great difference between the constitution of our Commonwealth and that of the Dominion of Canada, which is also a federation of states. By the Canadian constitution, certain powers are expressly reserved to the separate states; the power of the states is definitely limited to certain matters; and all the rest—the "residue of power," as it is called—is given to the central government. With us, it is exactly the reverse: it is the power of the central government that is definitely limited to certain matters, and the "residue of power" is left with the states. That is, the Commonwealth government can deal only with those matters which the constitution requires it to deal with; it must leave everything else for the states to deal with, as they did before federation came.

When states, then, come together in a federal union, it means that they hand over to a central government certain "matters of common concern," matters which concern all the states alike. When statesmen are drawing up a federal constitution, they have to ask themselves what these "matters of common concern" really are. They have, in fact, to ask two questions: *(a)* What are the things that can be better and more cheaply managed by one government than by several? *(b)* What things are likely, if left to be managed by the separate governments, to lead to quarrels between the states in the future? That is, you may look at federation in two ways: as a means of securing the greatest possible efficiency of management, and as a means of securing harmony and good-will between the states.

(In South Africa, a few years ago, certain wise and far-seeing men perceived that there were certain matters which, if left to the separate states to manage each in its own way, would inevitably lead to bitter disputes and probably to war. They had had some experience of the unspeakable horrors of war, and they were anxious to make impossible a repetition of those horrors. Therefore they strove hard to persuade the various states of South Africa to unite; and at last they succeeded. United South Africa is the sixth great federation of the modern world.)[4]

Carefully attending to those two questions, the statesmen who drew up our Commonwealth constitution determined that certain matters were "matters of common concern;" and when the Australian people accepted the constitution, what they really did was to agree that those matters should be handed over to a central authority, and taken out of the hands of the separate states.

To make this quite clear, let us look at one or two of the matters which were handed over to the Commonwealth, and at one or two which were not handed over. The Post-office, it was held, could be managed far better and more cheaply by one central authority than by six separate authorities; therefore the Post-office is a department of the Commonwealth government. But the Railways were left to the separate states; it was held (rightly or wrongly) that the Parliament of each state would know better how to manage the railways of that state, because it would be better acquainted with local requirements.

4   *Strictly speaking, South Africa is a unitary state, not a federation at all; the Union Parliament being legally supreme.*

Again, when a country is attacked by an enemy, it is above all things necessary that that country should act unitedly; therefore *Defence* was made a matter for the Commonwealth government to manage. But in *Education* it was held that there was no such urgent need for united action; that each state must determine how much education it can afford to pay for, and therefore that each state must be allowed to manage its own system of education. *Immigration* was clearly a matter for Commonwealth management, because it would be no use keeping undesirables out of New South Wales if Victoria allowed them to come in; that would be like putting a rabbit-proof fence half-way round a paddock. But the control of the undesirables who are already in Australia,—the prevention and punishment of crime,—was left to the separate states. *Public Health*, as we have seen, is a matter for separate states, and even for separate municipalities, to look after; but one matter which is of great importance to the public health, namely *Quarantine*, is dealt with by the Commonwealth. The states still raise money for their own needs by taxation; but one form of taxation—*customs duties*, the taxes on goods imported into Australia—was handed over to the Commonwealth; which was authorized to raise money by other kinds of taxation too, provided it imposed such taxation uniformly in all the states.

There is no need, at this point, to burden your memories with a complete list of the matters taken out of the control of the states and given to the Commonwealth to deal with; but there is need to warn you not to forget that, after all, the people who make up the states are the same people who make up the Commonwealth. This warning is necessary, because we read so much in our newspapers about disputes between the Commonwealth and the States, about the Commonwealth encroaching on the rights of the States, and so on, that we are really apt sometimes to forget for a moment that the people of the States *are* the people of the Commonwealth.

CHAPTER VII.

COMMONWEALTH AND EMPIRE.

Just as, if you are a member of any municipality in Australia, you are also a citizen of one of the Australian states; and just as, if you are a citizen of an Australian state, you must also be a citizen of the Australian Commonwealth; so, if you are a citizen of that Commonwealth, you are also a citizen of the British Empire. The Empire consists, as you know, first, of the United Kingdom; second, of the great self-governing Dominions,—Australia, New Zealand, Canada, and South Africa; third, of the great Dependency, India, to which self-government has not been granted; and, fourth, of a large number of smaller colonies and dependencies. Some of the smaller colonies are more or less completely self-governing; in one of them, the Leeward Islands, we find a federation.

Is the British Empire, then, itself a federation of Dominions, just as the Commonwealth is a federation of States? At first sight it looks as if Australia, Canada, and the rest might bear the same relation to the Empire as Victoria or New South Wales bear to the Commonwealth. But it is not so; and if you think for a moment you will see why it is not so. The people of Victoria or New South Wales choose their own state parliaments, but they also choose certain men to represent them in the Commonwealth parliament. If in like manner the Australian people chose men to represent them in the Imperial parliament, which meets in London, then indeed the British Empire would be a federation. But the Imperial parliament is chosen by the people of England, Ireland, Scotland, and Wales; Australia has no representatives in that parliament.

But then, you may ask, how can we be called a self-governing people, if we are governed by a parliament chosen by other people? How can we be said to govern ourselves, if the Imperial parliament, the supreme parliament of the Empire, the body which governs the Empire as a whole, contains no representatives chosen by us? To answer that question, we have to ask another: *Does* the Imperial parliament really govern the Empire as a whole?

Now the Constitution by which Australia is governed is, as we have seen, an Act of the Imperial parliament. Before we could federate, we had to get the Imperial parliament to make a law on the subject. The Imperial parliament gave Australia its constitution, as it had previously given each of the Australian states its constitution; but, having given those constitutions, it will never take them away, or alter them. Great Britain, having been taught a hard lesson by the American War of Independence, deliberately decided to confer upon her great colonies the power of governing themselves, and she has never dreamed of taking back her gift or any part of her gift. It is not necessary, in a little book like this, to speak of the *legal* powers of the Imperial parliament. About its legal powers let lawyers dispute; all we need trouble about is the power actually exercised; and we may say that the British parliament, in actual practice, could not—or at least would not—dream of interfering with our Commonwealth parliament, or with the parliament of any of the States, in its work of making laws, and carrying them out, for the "peace, order, and good government" of the people who have elected it.[5]

But there *are* certain matters which the Imperial parliament has not handed over to the parliaments of the Dominions. I have told

[5]   *Unless, that is, the right of self-government were so exercised as to bring about an international crisis which it would be dangerous for Britain to allow.*

you, on an earlier page, that "the Imperial governing body, sitting at Westminster, deals with matters which concern the Empire as a whole." The parliaments of the Dominions are not allowed to do things which would affect the safety and well-being of the whole Empire. The Commonwealth parliament could not sell or give away a part of Australia to a foreign power; it could not declare war upon a foreign power; it could not make an alliance with a foreign power. These things are left to the Imperial parliament; and naturally so, because at present it is the people of Great Britain who bear almost the whole of the enormous expense of defending the Empire. It is perfectly just that Great Britain, so long as she has to bear the burden of defending herself and her Empire, should take entire charge of the question of Peace and War, and the question of Foreign Relations, out of which war springs. Moreover, quite apart from the expense, a war affects not any one part of the Empire alone, but the Empire as a whole; it is absolutely necessary, therefore, that the matter of war should be left to a central authority, and not to the separate parts of the Empire.

But of late years the Dominions, including Australia, have seen it to be their duty to take a larger share in the burden of defending the Empire; and as the years go on, they will make larger and larger contributions to the common defence. Are they not bound to say, sooner or later, that since they pay a large amount towards the defence of the Empire, they ought to have a voice in determining how the money is to be used? Will they not ask to be consulted in questions of peace or war and foreign relations? In other words, will they not say that questions affecting the safety of the Empire as a whole ought to be dealt with by a new Parliament, to which all the Dominions send representatives? That would be Imperial Federation; and some people, even now, are wishing for, and working for, such a Parliament, because they believe that in it lies the only hope of permanent safety for the Empire; but the majority regard Imperial Federation as a wild dream. It is worth remembering, however, that majorities are not always right; and that wilder dreams than this have come true, when the dreamers have had the faith and the determination to *make* them come true.

CHAPTER VIII.

THE BRITISH EMPIRE.

The Empire of which Australia forms a part is very unlike any of the great Empires whose rise—and fall—we may read of in the pages of history. In saying this, I do not wish merely to remind you that ours is the *biggest* Empire the world has ever seen; that the King of no other nation has ever ruled over 400 millions of people; and that no other flag has ever waved, as the British flag waves, over 11½ million square miles—more than one-fifth of the total land area of the globe.

We may read, with wonder and with legitimate pride, the story of how British enterprise and courage and endurance have carried the flag to the ends of the earth, and added vast territories to the King's dominions; but it is not a good thing to be too boastful about all this. For the adding of vast territories does not bring greatness to a people, though it may bring opportunities of greatness.

> *It is not growing like a tree*
> *In bulk, doth make man better be.*

The mere size of a man is no guarantee of his soundness in body or in mind; and the mere size of the British Empire is no sign that it is not suffering from the same diseases as the great empires of the past have suffered from, no sign that it will not be swept away as they were swept away, and all its greatness crumble into dust. Happily, there are other and far more important differences than the difference in size.

If we look at one of the mighty empires of the past—at the

Roman Empire, for example—we find the ruling state, the master of the whole empire, sending out soldiers and tax-gatherers to the various provinces of the empire; soldiers to keep the conquered peoples in order, and tax-gatherers to wring as much money out of them as they could be made to pay. We find one state ruling, with a rod of iron, a number of subject peoples; peoples held together by force; peoples united to one another by no bond of nationality, or of language, or of religion; united only by the fact that the one imperial sword held them all in awe, and the one imperial master plundered them. If we turn from this picture and look at the bonds which tie the great self-governing dominions to one another and to the United Kingdom, we see at once that the British Empire is not an empire at all, in the old sense of the word. Britain is not our imperial master. She sends no tax-gatherers to wring money from us; and if she sends us soldiers, it is not to keep us in order but to keep us in safety. The British people have always reverenced liberty, as the essential condition of true well-being. It was for liberty that they fought, first against the tyranny of kings, and then against the tyranny of a ruling class. It was their belief in liberty that made them, first of all the nations, insist that slavery should not be allowed to exist anywhere in their territory; and it was this same belief in liberty that made them grant self-government to their colonies—or at least to such of their colonies as seemed fit to manage their own affairs. Under the protection of the British flag, but without interference from Britain, the young colonies have been allowed to grow up into strong, self-reliant peoples; and we now have the spectacle, not of a ruling nation imposing its will by force on subject peoples, but rather of a *sisterhood of nations*, united by various bonds and working together for various purposes. Such a sisterhood of nations is an empire the like of which has never before existed in this world.

A few years ago Britain had to engage in a long and costly war with the Boers of the Transvaal. Britain won; the Boers were forced to become British subjects. Four years later, Britain gave self-government to the Transvaal; and that, too, without asking the conquered people to pay a penny of the millions of pounds which the war had cost, and without asking them to pay a penny towards the defence of the Empire in the future. Such a thing has never happened anywhere except in the British Empire.

It is as a sisterhood of free nations, then, that we are to think of the British Empire. The self-governing dominions—Australia, New Zealand, and the rest of us,—are growing up, and are becoming more and more conscious of their strength and their importance in the world; each of them is growing tired of being called a colony, and prefers to think of itself as a nation. We in Australia, for instance, do not nowadays speak of ourselves as colonials, inhabiting certain British colonies in Australia; we speak rather of the *Australian nation*, a new nation, with, as we hope, a splendid future of national greatness in front of it. And you will sometimes hear people speak as if this were a bad thing; as if the growing up of a new feeling of nationhood were likely to spoil our feeling of loyalty to the Empire. And you will hear other people speak as if loyalty to the Empire ought to be discouraged, being likely to prevent us from being patriotic Australians. Talk of this kind is foolish; loyalty to our own country and loyalty to the Empire are not opposed to one another; they go together, just as self-respect and respect for other people go together. If you ever go into business, and have to look for a partner, you will find that a man who respects himself is the very best kind of partner to have; and so it is with that partnership of nations which we call the British Empire. The two kinds of loyalty have grown up together; while we have been learning to think of ourselves as a separate nation, we have also been learning to think that the united Empire has a greater and more glorious destiny in store for it than could possibly be achieved by any of the Dominions acting separately. While the new sense of nationhood has been growing, there has been growing also a new sense of the *oneness* of the Empire.

At the present time this phrase—"the oneness of the Empire"—has a very real meaning for every Australian. We talk of a sisterhood of free nations; but how long would Australia remain a free nation if Britain lost the power of helping us to keep our freedom? Let one decisive battle be fought at the other side of the world,—let the British Navy suffer defeat in the North Sea,—and our freedom to govern ourselves would go down like a child's castle of cards; the foreign power that had beaten Britain could go round the Empire and help itself to what it chose. We are building an Australian navy; but is there any one so far-sighted that he can descry the time when our Australian navy will, *alone*, be a match for the stupendous strength of one of the great European powers? All the blessings that spring from freedom and self-government—and they are many—come to us through the fact that we are a part of the British Empire.

Britain is finding it difficult to bear the enormous and daily increasing burden of defending the Empire; we shall see, when we come to the chapter on "Defence," how enormous that burden is. The day may come—though we all hope it never will—when Britain, beset by powerful foes, will be in dire need of help, and will call upon the young Dominions to aid her. Against that day it is the duty of the Dominions to strengthen themselves and be ready. For many years they did not face that duty, but they are facing it now in earnest, and in so doing they are showing the world what "the oneness of the Empire" means.

There, then, is one reason—a selfish reason it may seem—why we should be glad that we belong to the British Empire; but there are other and less selfish reasons. It is no empty boast to say that Britain has been, and is, one of the greatest powers for good that the world has ever seen. We may say—not in a braggart spirit, but soberly and quietly, remembering many shortcomings and many blunders,—that the British Empire has used its mighty strength in the cause of justice, of liberty, of happiness,—of civilization, in a word. And if you ask me to give a definite example of this, I will speak of one other point of difference between the British Empire and all the other empires that have ever existed; and that is in their treatment of subject races.

Besides the self-governing peoples of the Empire, there are, as you know, millions of dark-skinned subjects of the King, who have not been thought fit for the gift of self-government. Now in any of the great empires of the past these conquered races would have been looked upon as people to *exploit*, people to make money out of. (Look, for instance, at the history of the Spanish Empire, and see how Spain dealt with the natives of South America.) No other empire has ever regarded it as a duty to govern the subject races in the interests, not of the conquerors, but of the conquered. Greedy British traders may, indeed, have tried to enrich themselves by the labour of the native races; but Britain has always set her face against such plundering; she has always thought the good government of the conquered people a task entrusted to her. There is no space here to tell you the marvellous story of how Britain has governed India, with its teeming population of 294 millions, of many races, many languages, and many religions; how she has brought order to these people, preventing the stronger races from trampling on the weaker; how she has brought them justice, which treats rich and poor alike; how she has helped them to escape from poverty; how she has brought vast stores of food to whatever part of the country was threatened by famine; how she has built hospitals to heal their diseases, schools to enlighten their ignorance, and universities to continue what the schools had begun; how, finally, she has breathed into the souls of these dark peoples something of her own deep passion for liberty, so that they are now beginning to demand the power to govern themselves. In that country, British rule has been an endeavour to turn warfare into peace, ignorance into knowledge, oppression into justice, and widespread misery into general comfort and contentment. No-one who studies the history of British India will fail to see that there, at least, Britain has been a great civilizing power; and so she has been in other parts of the world.

That is one reason, among many, why we ought to feel proud that we are members of the British Empire, privileged to take our part in its work, to be sharers of its duties and partakers of its strength.

PART II.
THE WORK OF GOVERNMENT.

In the foregoing pages, you have read about government in general, and about the different "governing bodies" whose work touches the life of every Australian man, woman, and child. It might seem natural now to go on and tell you what these governing bodies are like, how they are constructed, and how they do their work; to describe, in fact, the machinery of government. But it is hard to take an interest in the construction of a machine before we know what the machine is for, what work it does, what products it turns out; and therefore, before telling you about parliament and the rest of the machinery of government, I shall speak of some—not by any means all—of the kinds of work which government does for us.

CHAPTER IX.

PUBLIC HEALTH.

Government is the means by which society seeks to help every individual citizen to live the best possible kind of life. In other words, government exists to preserve and to increase the well-being of the citizens. Therefore, it is the duty of government to do battle every day and all day long with the great enemies of human well-being, among which the chief are disease, ignorance, vice, and poverty.

Now these four enemies of the human race are closely related to one another; they are four brothers, and they always assist one another. For instance: disease is often the result of ignorance; vice is often the result of poverty; ignorance is often the result of poverty; poverty is often the result of disease; and so on. Thus, to fight against one of these is to fight against all the rest; when we win a victory over ignorance, we win a victory over disease and vice and poverty as well.

Now these enemies attack each of us separately, and each of us separately has got to do battle with them; no government can relieve us of that responsibility. The best government in the world cannot prevent you from being a drunkard or a pauper, if you have no strength of will of your own. The best government in the world cannot make you virtuous or well-informed, if you have not the will to seek virtue and knowledge. What government can do is to help us in our warfare with these enemies, one or other of whom would probably, but for this help, be too strong for most of us. The mean-

THE VICTORIAN QUARANTINE STATION.

ing of this will be made clear, if we think about what government does in the way of helping us to fight disease.

I take this enemy first, because good health is the very foundation of all well-being. Great things have been done by men who were physically weak and diseased; some people have wills strong enough to triumph over ill-health. But, for the great majority of us, strength of will and strength of mind depend on strength and soundness of body. And in various ways government helps us all to keep our bodies sound and strong. Government seeks to protect the public health in two ways: first, by the prevention of disease; second, by the curing of it.

In the first place, government stands as a sentry at our outer gates—our sea-ports—and tries to prevent infectious diseases from coming into the Commonwealth. When a steamer from Europe arrives at its first Australian port, a doctor in the service of the government goes on board, and inspects the passengers, and receives a report from the steamer's doctor. If he finds one of the passengers suffering from an infectious disease—small-pox, for instance—then that vessel is *quarantined*; none of its passengers is allowed to land in Australia, except to go into a "quarantine station," where they are detained until all danger of infection is over; and steps are taken to prevent the disease from being carried into our country by the cargo. This is called the quarantine system; and it is because we have a good quarantine system that various infectious diseases common in Europe and Asia, such as hydrophobia[6], have never managed to gain a footing in Australia.

But it is not enough to prevent the introduction of infectious disease from outside; infectious diseases break out in our midst, and it is necessary to prevent them from spreading from one part of the country to another, and even from one house to another. For

6   Hydrophobia is the old term for the fearful spasms and difficulty swallowing that occur in the later stages of rabies; it refers to a symptom, not the disease itself.

this purpose, a law has been made, in each of the states, declaring certain diseases "notifiable"; that is to say, when anyone is found to be suffering from one of these diseases—small-pox, for example, or diphtheria, or scarlet fever, or typhoid, or bubonic plague—the doctor attending the patient is bound to give notice of the fact to an officer of government, who, in his turn, is bound to take all possible steps to prevent the disease from spreading; he may even, if he thinks it necessary, isolate the house in which the disease has broken out, forbidding anyone to leave it or to enter it, until the danger of infection is over. This may seem hard on those who live in that house; but government has to think, not of the convenience of one particular household, but of the safety of the whole community.

But prevention of the spread of disease is only one small part of the government's task; it has to try to prevent disease from occurring. To do this, it has to enforce certain standards of cleanliness; for with all the care in the world it is impossible to do much against disease in a filthy city. Unfortunately some people, if left to themselves, would allow their houses to be always filthy and their backyards to be breeding-grounds of disease. Such people are a perpetual danger to the health of their neighbours; in the interests of public health, government has to step in and compel them to observe a certain standard of cleanliness.

In this way government prevents the private individual from endangering, by his carelessness or ignorance, the health of the whole community. But government has to fight against more than carelessness and ignorance; it has to fight against unscrupulous greed of money—the greed which will tempt a man to sell diseased meat or tainted milk to unsuspecting customers. In most of the Australian states there are laws (such as the *Pure Food* Acts in New South Wales and Victoria, and the *Food and Drugs Act* in South Australia) by which government is able to stop people from selling impure or otherwise harmful foods and drugs to the public. The importance of this is perhaps most clearly seen in the case of milk. Milk, which is an invaluable food for children, may, if the persons who handle it are careless or dirty, be turned into the deadliest poison; indeed, it is probable that more children have died from what is called "milk poisoning" than from any other cause whatsoever. Therefore government has directed special attention to the milk supply. It punishes anyone who is found selling milk that has been watered or adulterated in any way, milk that is not clean and fresh and wholesome; and it sends inspectors to the dairies, to see that they are kept clean and that the cows are healthy.

Again, the protection of public health makes it necessary that every town should have a clean, cheap, and abundant water-supply; clean, that we may be able to drink it freely without risk of disease; cheap and abundant, that even the poorest may have no excuse for neglecting the duty of cleanliness. The water-supply, therefore, is a matter which government takes in hand. And government also undertakes the task, the right performance of which is absolutely essential to the public health, of providing a proper system of drainage for every town, however small. It overcomes, too, what has been in the past a fruitful cause of disease, by providing for the proper burial of the dead.

There are certain industries, the workers engaged in which are peculiarly liable to contract certain diseases; mining is one terrible example. Where the danger can be averted by proper precautions, it is the duty of government to compel the employer to take those precautions; and, in general, it may be said that government has done much to make it impossible for any employer to conduct his industry with reckless indifference to the health of his employees. That work in mine, factory, and workshop is not more unhealthy than it is is due, to a large extent, to government interference in defence of the workers' health.

By providing many large public parks and gardens, and by car-

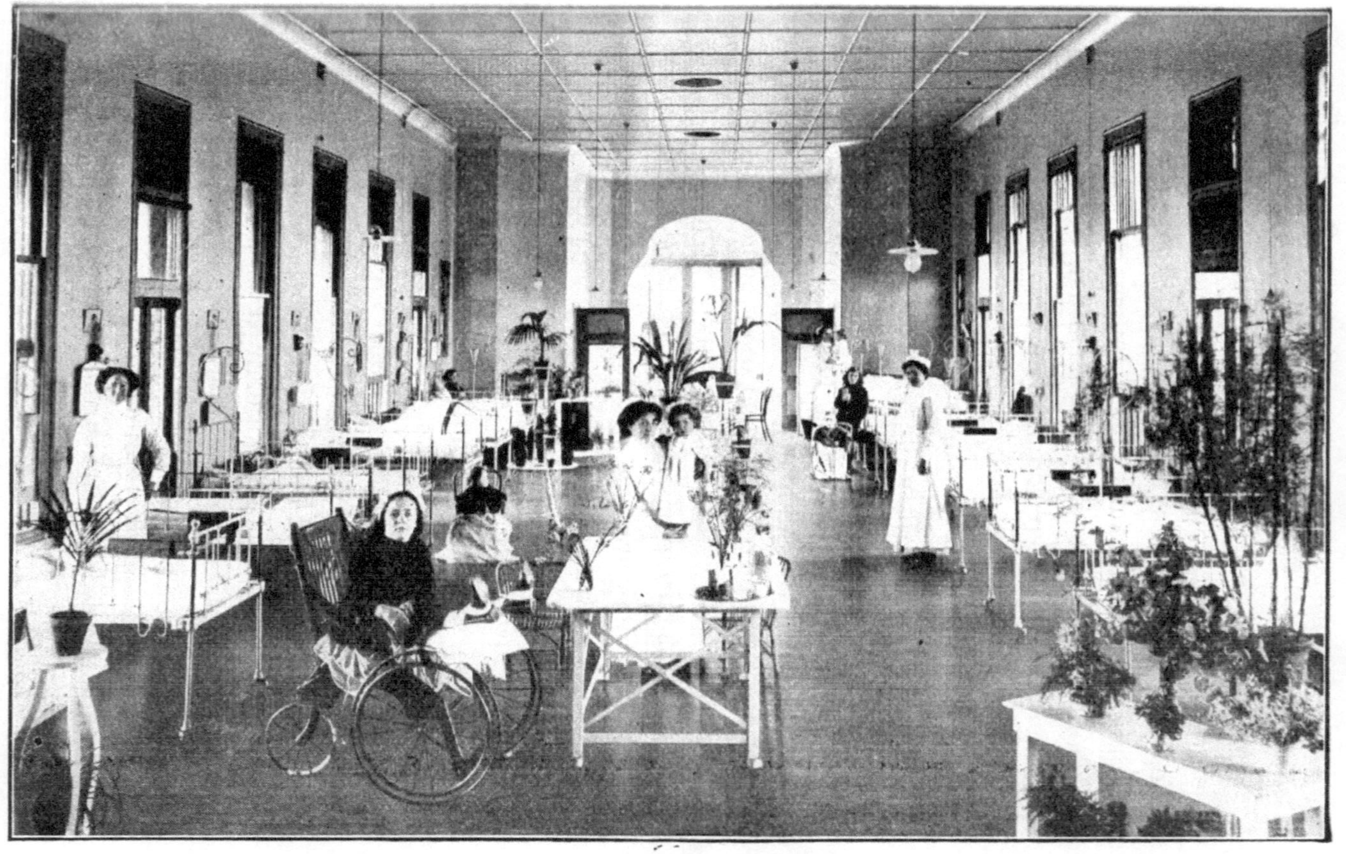

IN A CHILDREN'S HOSPITAL.

rying people at cheap rates on the railways to the country or to the seaside, government does a great deal for the prevention of disease; for recreation in the open-air is one of the best safeguards of health. And the workers of Australia have shorter hours of labour, and therefore more abundant leisure for recreation, than the workers of most other countries; they have also more numerous holidays. And the climate, in the greater part of Australia, is so fine that we can all spend a great deal of our leisure time in the open-air. It is a pity that so many people do not yet know how to use their leisure in a healthy way. To watch other people playing a game, when you might be playing it yourself, is scarcely to be called a real recreation; and to stand all the afternoon roaring yourself hoarse at a football match seems neither a sensible nor a healthful way of spending a holiday; it is almost as stupid as hanging about the streets doing nothing. The surest way of fighting a disease is to begin by discovering the cause of it; and most modern governments spend large sums of money in keeping up laboratories, in which men are continually trying to discover the causes of various diseases.

Though, during the last twenty years, enormous strides have been made in this matter of preventing disease, still, of course, disease does in innumerable cases baffle all attempts at prevention; and when prevention has failed, we have to think about cure. There are at least two very important ways in which government helps us to cure our diseases. In the first place, it protects us against those most dangerous persons, the quack doctor and the untrained chemist. It insists that nobody shall be allowed to practise those professions who does not hold a certificate showing that he or she has had a proper training for the work; and this is of great importance for the public health. In the second place, government either provides or helps to provide public hospitals, at which the sick are attended to by skilful doctors at a very small cost, or even free of charge altogether if they are too poor to pay anything. It provides also special hospitals for infectious diseases, for incurable invalids, for the insane, for the blind, for the deaf and dumb.

Much will be done in the future, both for the prevention and for the cure of disease, by the new system of inspection of schools by a government medical officer. Tasmania has the honour of having been the first Australian state to introduce this excellent system.

In this chapter I have used the word "government" a great many times; and you may naturally ask, What government is meant,—local government, or state government, or Commonwealth government? The answer is, all of them; the public health is so important a matter, that they all play their parts in protecting it. The drainage of a town, for instance, is as a rule left to the local governing body to look after; the sale of impure foods is dealt with by the state government—which, however, hands over many of its duties to a kind of committee, called the Board of Public Health; while the quarantine system is managed by the Commonwealth government, it being felt that this is a matter which can be far better dealt with by one central authority than by six separate authorities.

There are two points which you ought to notice about this great public battle with disease. In the first place, government does things for us which we could not possibly do for ourselves as private individuals. You could keep your own backyard clean, no doubt, but you could not compel your neighbours to keep theirs clean; you could not drain the whole town, so as to make it a healthy place for you to live in; you could not prevent people who are suffering from infectious diseases from travelling in the trains and endangering your health; you could not, by your own unaided efforts, do one-millionth part of all that is done to guard you from sickness. Here, then, is one of your great debts to society; society, by means of its machine called government, fights in defence of your health.

The second point is this. You have heard in this chapter a good deal about compulsion. Government *compels* people to keep their premises clean; it *compels* employers to consider the health of those who work for them; it *compels* dairymen to sell only pure milk; and so on. Amid so much compulsion, you may ask, What becomes of liberty? Is not government, in all these cases, interfering with liberty? The answer is—Certainly; government does, and must, interfere with liberty, if by liberty you mean liberty to do things which are likely to injure other people. Society cannot afford to grant its members one shred of that kind of liberty,—the kind of liberty which would destroy or injure or endanger the well-being of society itself.

Though much is done in this matter, much still remains to do. "Australia," says Professor Osborne, "loses every year more lives through *preventable* disease than would be left on the battlefield after a humiliating defeat by a foreign power; and as it is our duty to defend the country from hostile armaments, so we must defend it from more subtle and more deadly foes, who have no respect for red cross or white flag."

CHAPTER X.

PUBLIC EDUCATION.

In the last chapter, we saw how government fights for us against that dread enemy of the human race, disease; in this, we are going to look at its perpetual warfare with a second enemy,—ignorance. Its chief weapon, in this great fight, is called Public Education. In ancient times, it was not looked upon as part of the duty of the state to educate its citizens; the matter was left in private hands. And in the Middle Ages, the task was mainly performed by the Church. But in modern times, the feeling has gradually grown up, in all civilized countries, that the education of the people is a thing of boundless importance to the general well-being; that it ought to be treated as public work, and provided for out of the public money,—the money raised by taxation; in other words, that it is one of the duties of government. And almost all modern governments have accepted the task, and look upon it as one of the most important they are called upon to perform.

In every Australian state, education is *free and compulsory*. That is to say, the state provides a school education, free of charge, for all its children; and it insists that every child shall take advantage of this provision,—that every child in the state shall be educated; if not in one of the schools provided by the state, then elsewhere. Perhaps it will be as well to give one or two of the reasons why we have come to look upon education as a thing so vitally important that we insist on everyone being educated.

(1.) The Australian states, as we have seen, are self-governing; every Australian citizen who has reached the age of twenty-one is allowed a vote, which means a voice in governing the country. But this would be a terrible power to entrust to uneducated persons; self-government in the hands of a mass of ignorant people would be as dangerous as a loaded gun in the hands of an infant. Ignorant persons cannot even manage their own affairs wisely; how then are they to be expected to manage wisely the affairs of the nation? The supreme need, for a self-governing state, is the need of a body of enlightened and thoughtful citizens; men and women trained to reflect, to reason, and to observe; trained also to be masters of themselves, to control their passions, to do their duty. (2.) Education is the best way of improving the material prosperity of the country. An uneducated community is a poor community. In Russia, at the present time, more than three-quarters of the population are unable to read or write; and in Russia there is such a widespread and degrading poverty as we in Australia, happily, find it hard to imagine. The greatness of a nation does not mean its material prosperity; but a certain measure of material prosperity is a necessary condition of true national greatness. (3.) One of the chief duties of government is to preserve public order,—to protect all its citizens against violence and lawlessness. But ignorance is the mother of disorder; violence and lawlessness flourish where education is neglected; for education, remember, means a training of the character as well as of the intellect. (4.) Our sense of justice tells us that all children born into this world ought to have an equal start, an equal chance at the beginning of their lives, an equal opportunity of making the best of themselves. We feel it to be unjust that a child, who has done no wrong, should be punished because his parents are poor, and condemned to lead a life of unintelligent drudgery simply because his parents have not been able to give him a good start. No government has ever yet succeeded in doing away with the inequalities of fortune; but a long stride is made towards equality and justice when government provides, for the children even of the poorest, the best education it can. (5.) As we have seen, good government aims at helping all the citizens to lead the best kind of life possible to them. Among civilized nations, there is a general feeling that knowledge and wisdom are elements in the "best kind of life;" that a life deprived of knowledge is an incomplete and stunted life; that the ancient sage spoke words of eternal truth when he said—"Wisdom is the principal thing; therefore get wisdom; and with all thy getting get understanding."

These are a few of the reasons why we have come to look upon the education of the people as one of the chief duties of government. But until quite recent times, it was thought—in Britain and also in Australia—that the only kind of education which government ought to provide, the only kind of education which ought to be compulsory and also free, was what is called *primary* education; it was even thought by some people that government had done its whole duty towards children when it had taught them reading, writing, and the simple rules of arithmetic. And you must not despise this elementary kind of education; for a person who has once learned to read has in his hands the key, not to all knowledge, but to all that vast treasure-house of knowledge which is to be found in books. Primary education, however, goes much farther than this, as you know; the primary schools provide teaching in history, geography, nature-study, and other subjects.

But nowadays, in all the most civilized countries, including Australia, it is thought that the duty of the state in the matter of education does not end with primary education; it is thought that for the sake of the general welfare, the state ought to go much farther than this. And so, in every one of the Australian states, government makes provision for the continued education of those who have learned all that the primary school can teach them. When a pupil leaves the primary school he is not yet fit to enter the University or one of the highest technical schools; to be fit for this, he must receive what is called a *secondary* education; and government provides this secondary education by means of schools known by various names: superior schools, high schools, continuation schools, higher elementary schools, agricultural high schools, and so on; also by giving scholarships which enable those who win them to receive a secondary education, free of charge, from a private school.

Then, beyond secondary education, comes what is known as the higher education: that is, the education given at universities, technical colleges, and training colleges.

The Australian university system is a thing which has grown up gradually; New South Wales founded her university so long ago as 1852; it was not till 1911 that Western Australia decided to have one. At the university, the student may pursue his general education, studying history and philosophy, literature and foreign languages; or he may study various sciences; or he may be trained for what are sometimes called the "learned professions,"—law, medicine, and engineering; or he may study the art of teaching. University education is neither compulsory nor free; but it is not very expensive, and the fees paid by the students are not nearly sufficient to pay for the carrying on of these costly institutions; government has to step in and help them. The government of Victoria, for instance, pays more than £20,000 every year towards the carrying on of the University of Melbourne.

The higher technical colleges give an advanced training in various kinds of industry; their business is to turn out skilled workmen. As the prosperity of the country largely depends on its supply of skilled workmen, this is a most important branch of education; hitherto it has not received, in Australia, anything like the attention it deserves, but the near future will see a great development in technical education. The Working Men's College, in Melbourne, is a good example

A WOODWORK CLASS, PERTH, W.A.

of what is meant by a technical college; other examples are the various Schools of Mines and Agricultural Colleges.

Then there are the training colleges for teachers. Teaching is a delicate and difficult art, and to be a good teacher requires a long and severe training. If government is to provide a good education, it must provide an army of well-trained teachers; accordingly, in almost all of the Australian states, there is a training college for this purpose. In some of the states the necessary training is given partly at this college, partly at the university.

On primary education alone, the Australian states, between them, spend nearly three million pounds every year. This seems a very large sum, but remember that, besides paying salaries to an army of more than 16,000 teachers, a great deal of money has to be spent on school buildings. For a good education, good buildings are necessary; the health of the pupils requires that they shall not spend their school hours in close, small, dark rooms.

Besides the schools provided by the states, there are some 2,000 private schools in Australia, many of them giving both a primary and a secondary education. Until lately, it was thought that the duty of government, with regard to private schools, was to let them alone; but we are gradually coming to see that it is absurd to insist that every child shall attend a school unless we also insist that every school shall give a real education; and that it is just as necessary for government to protect the public against ignorant, untrained, and unskilful teachers as against ignorant, untrained, and unskilful doctors. Accordingly, in Victoria and Tasmania a law has been made, which will ultimately have the effect of preventing anyone from teaching in a school who has not received a proper training; in Western Australia, too, government tries to exercise some supervision over private schools.

But government provides education for the people by other means besides schools and colleges and universities. Public libraries, museums, and art galleries are educational institutions. In each of the capital cities of Australia there is a large public library, the largest—at Sydney—containing over 200,000 books; and there are smaller libraries in all the important towns. And in many other ways government tries to help the citizens to acquire knowledge.

Now in this warfare which government wages with public ignorance, there are two things which it is worth while pointing out. The first is that you must not say—"Well, I, at any rate, owe nothing to government in this matter; my parents were rich enough to send me to a private school, so that I would have received an education in any case, without any help from government." What! do you think your welfare is affected only by *your own* education, and not at all by other people's?—that your life would be just the same if you had to live among ignorant savages? No: we are social beings, and that means that the character of our life is coloured by the character of the community amid which we live. It is an immense advantage to you to live in the midst of an educated community; and if it had not been for the help of the government, only a very small fraction of the community would ever have been educated.

In the second place, we have noticed that in the matter of education, as in the matter of public health, government exercises compulsion; parents are compelled to send their children to school. Here, once more, we are perhaps inclined to think that liberty is being interfered with. But this is really a very good example of the way in which one kind of liberty may be sacrificed in order that a much greater and finer kind of liberty may be gained. Government, you say, in compelling us to acquire knowledge whether we want to or not, is playing the part of a tyrant? What government really does is to set us free from a tyrant—one of the worst tyrants that ever oppressed humanity, a tyrant who has enslaved whole nations more cruelly than any mere human tyrant could ever do,—the tyrant whose name is Ignorance.

CHAPTER XI.

PUBLIC ORDER.

The next great enemy of human happiness, and the deadliest of all, is vice; and all good government fights against it with various weapons. One of these weapons is education; for all vice is a defect of character, and education, as we have seen, aims at improving the character as well as the intellect. Sometimes government attacks vice more directly; as, for instance, by the liquor laws which, in each Australian state, are used as a means of coping with the vice of intemperance. When we strike a blow at drunkenness we strike at the root of a whole host of vices; we strike, too, at one of the roots of poverty.

But, for the most part, government does not attempt, except indirectly by means of education, to prevent vice; but it does strive with all its might to prevent crime, which is the outcome of vice. It cannot do very much to prevent a man from being vicious; but it can and does do a great deal to prevent the vicious man from indulging his vice to the injury of others. It cannot prevent me from being greedy; but it can prevent me from indulging my greed by stealing another man's property. It cannot prevent me from being bad-tempered; but it can prevent me from indulging my bad temper to the extent of assaulting someone whom I happen to have quarrelled with. Or, if it cannot prevent me from committing these crimes, it can punish me severely when I have committed them, and so prevent others from acting in the same way.

The subject of this chapter, then, is not the prevention of vice,

AN AUSTRALIAN POLICEMAN

with which government has little to do; but the prevention of crime—or, in other words, the maintenance of Public Order,—which is everywhere looked upon as one of the first duties of government.

It is only in modern times, as we have seen, that public education has been looked upon as a task that government ought to perform; and the idea that government ought in every possible way to protect the public health may almost be called a new idea. It is quite otherwise with the maintenance of public order; this has been looked upon as the duty of government ever since civilization began. For a long time, indeed, this was looked upon as the only duty of government, as the one thing for which government existed: to protect the life and property of the citizen against violence and crime, to prevent disorder, to keep "the King's peace" throughout the land. We do not nowadays look on this as the only duty of government, but we still regard it as a most important duty; and we think it the surest sign of a strong government, when this duty is thoroughly done.

Here in Australia, you walk along any road, in city or country, with a perfect feeling of safety; you have no fear of being set upon by a murderer or a bushranger. You own a piece of land at the other end of the Commonwealth; you have no fear that, because you are absent, someone else will seize your land and refuse to give it back. You lie down to sleep at night with perfect ease of mind; you are not afraid that in the middle of the night a band of your enemies will attack your house. It seems absurd even to imagine such things; we are so accustomed to the feeling of security that we take it for granted, and never think of all that it means. But try to fancy what it would be like to be a member of a savage tribe, such as exist even at the present moment in uncivilized parts of the world; living always in the midst of alarms, seeing in every stranger a possible enemy, suspecting almost everyone you met of designs against your life or your property, knowing that your only protection was your own strength and cunning, and knowing well that your chief, or any man more powerful than yourself, could do with you exactly as he pleased. Try to form a clear idea of what that would be like, and then you will appreciate the difference between that life and the life you actually lead in Australia. Well, the difference is mainly due to the fact that in Australia we have a government strong enough to maintain order, to protect us from crime and violence. When Englishmen praised William the Conqueror for "the good peace he made in the land, so that a man might fare over his realm with a bosom full of gold," they were praising him for the strong government he had given them; stern as he was, cruel as they thought him, they saw that at any rate he was able to maintain order throughout his kingdom; and they knew so well what violence and disorder meant, that they felt supremely grateful to him. We, today, scarcely know what violence and disorder mean; but if the strong hand of government were removed, we should soon know.

Among our distant ancestors, when they were only just beginning to be civilized, an injury done by one man to another was a private matter. If a man did you a wrong, you tried to avenge that wrong by yourself, or with the aid of your friends. If someone was murdered, his family and friends endeavoured to take vengeance upon the murderer, if they could catch him. But nowadays, if a man does you an injury, and in so doing breaks the law, it is no longer a private matter; the state takes up your cause for you. If a man breaks the lock of your safe and steals your money, it is not you, but the state, that must endeavour to catch him and punish him and restore the money. He has broken something much more sacred than the lock of your safe; he has broken the law; and he has against him the whole strength of government, whose duty it is to guard the laws.

Government keeps order, prevents crime, makes law prevail over lawlessness, chiefly by means of that body of public servants known as the *police force*. The policeman, with his blue coat and his oddly shaped helmet and his shining buttons, is a very familiar figure in our streets; but, familiar as he is, we shall always look at him with respect if we remember what he stands for—the strong right arm of government. Law, as we shall see, is the great protector of all our liberties; and the policeman is the guardian of the law. There are several ways in which he performs the duty of keeping order.

In the first place, it is his task to "keep the peace," or prevent public disturbance. In times of great public discontent or public excitement, crowds sometimes become riotous and do violent things, committing crimes against property and even against life. This the policeman has to try to prevent. He attends meetings where disorder is feared, breaks up street crowds which threaten to become disorderly, and stops disorderly crowds, if he can, from breaking the law. Sometimes, of course, a riot goes so far that the police cannot cope with it; then government may have to call in the aid of the soldiers. But public disturbances of the peace are a very rare occurrence in Australia; we are, on the whole, a law-abiding people.

Secondly, the policeman prevents crime by keeping his eye on the people who are likely to commit crimes. In every great city there is a small class of "habitual criminals,"—men who have been imprisoned, perhaps many times, for the crimes they have committed, who have been let out of prison, and who are almost sure to commit another crime if they see a chance of doing so. The criminal is greatly kept in check by his knowledge that the policemen have their eye on him, know where he lives, watch his goings and comings, and are well aware of his character. There would be an immensely greater number of crimes committed every year, if the police did not keep an unsleeping watch on these enemies of society. The policemen are society's watchdogs.

Thirdly, when a crime has been committed, it is the policeman's duty to find and arrest the criminal as quickly as possible. Often, of course, the criminal escapes from the scene of his crime and leaves behind him nothing to show who has committed it; in that case, the services of a special kind of policeman may be required,—the detective, whose special business it is to detect the authors of crimes and to track them to wherever they may be hiding. This is not always possible, for criminals are very cunning; and many crimes go unpunished for this reason. But the detective is often wonderfully skilful; and much crime is prevented by the fact that evil-doers know that they are almost certain to be found out. When the policeman has caught the criminal, his task is ended; it is no part of his duty to punish the criminal. It is a fundamental part of our law, that no-one shall be punished except after a fair trial; and the policeman has nothing to do with trying the criminal; this is the work of the Law Courts, which will be the subject of a later chapter. You remember the names of the three different organs of government—legislature, executive, and judiciary. The policeman, as servant of the executive, catches the criminal, and hands him over to the judiciary. The judiciary tries him, and, if he is found guilty, fixes the kind and amount of punishment he is to receive. Then he is handed back to the executive, which inflicts that punishment upon him. The management of prisons belongs to the work of government on its executive side.

Thus government—by means of its servants, the police—tries to prevent crimes from being committed; and when it cannot prevent them from being committed, it punishes those who have committed them. But punishment is also a means of prevention; crimes would be ten times as numerous as they are, if evil-intentioned people did not know that punishment follows the breaking of the law. Just above what we call the criminal class is the far larger class of men who would be violent and lawless and disorderly if they dared; these are continually kept in check by their knowledge that government has a sword in its hand, and will strike, if need be, strongly, swiftly, and relentlessly.

As we have noticed already, the punishment of crime was once looked on as a private matter; it is now a public matter; government not only punishes the law-breaker, but refuses to allow him to be punished by any private individual. What is called "taking the law into one's own hands" is itself a crime. In some of the southern states of America, for example, "lynching" is not uncommon: when a murder has been committed, a number of private citizens will sometimes seize the person whom they suspect of the crime, and, after a very rough trial, or without any trial at all, they will hang him. To us it seems that lynching is simply murder. Where lynching occurs, it is a sure sign that the government is weak,—too weak to maintain order; a sure sign, too, that in the hearts of the citizens there is little of that reverence for law upon which the peace and well-being of society rest.

Keeping order is the most important duty of government; for government could not perform any of its other tasks if it were not strong enough to keep order. There may be order without liberty; but there cannot be any real liberty, for the majority of people, without order. In a country where violence prevails, where life is insecure, where the strong trample on the weak, where the only law is

> *That he shall take who has the power,*
> *And he shall keep who can,—*

in such a country there can be no real liberty; neither can there be any real progress in civilization. Education, commerce, manufactures, literature, science, all the arts and inventions that have helped to make life enjoyable,—all rest on a foundation of order. Happily, the keeping of order is not so difficult a task in Australia as in many countries; for we have inherited British traditions, and have learned, almost in our cradles, lessons of discipline, of obedience to law, of hatred of violence, and love of order.

CHAPTER XII.

PREVENTION OF POVERTY.

Though we may include poverty among the four great enemies of human happiness, we must not fall into the stupid mistake of thinking that in order to be really happy one must contrive to grow rich; that well-being consists in being able to eat costly foods, drink costly wines, wear splendid clothes, live in a magnificent house, drive abroad in a gorgeous motor-car, and have innumerable servants to do one's bidding. Doubtless many a rich man has found out by sad experience that wealth is after all not worth striving for, and that the very best things in life, the things that make life worth living, are just the things that no amount of money will buy; such things as love, and friendship, and health, and peace of mind. That is true; and yet it is equally true that poverty is one of the greatest enemies of human well-being. Though riches may not be able to buy happiness for us, extreme poverty assuredly condemns us to misery. There is a "poverty-line" below which a man cannot sink without losing all that is worth calling happiness; and it is the sad truth that millions of people, even in the British Empire, live below that line. Extreme poverty,—poverty which grinds a man down and chokes all that is best in him, which starves him physically and degrades him morally, which robs him of strength in the present and of hope for the future,—no argument can make such poverty appear anything but a deadly evil. A man who, by his fault or by his misfortune, has sunk into this condition, is a man whose whole existence is made wretched by want and fear; want of the very necessaries of life, sufficient food, warmth, shelter, and clothing; and fear of losing his employment, with consequent starvation for himself and his wife and children. He has no prospect of bettering himself; he looks into the future and sees in front of him years of hard, monotonous, unceasing toil; and, for the reward of his toil, "a life of unsuccessful battling with hunger, rounded by a pauper's grave." If such a man becomes brutalised, if he tries to drown his wretchedness in drink, can anyone be surprised? He is deprived of the thing which human beings need more than they need anything else; he is deprived of hope.

> *No hope of more or better*
> *This side the hungry grave;*
> *Till death release the debtor,*
> *Eternal sleep the slave.*

Plainly, if government is going to aim at enabling every citizen to live "the best kind of life," it must fight with all its strength against such poverty as this.

But, you will say, in Australia we have no such dire poverty as this, or very little; and it will be easy to prevent its ever becoming common in a country so rich and fertile as ours is. Do not let us deceive ourselves; a country may be very wealthy, and yet have enormous masses of desperately poor people in it. Great Britain is, in proportion to its population, the richest country in the whole world; and yet, of the 43,000,000 inhabitants of Great Britain, no fewer than 38,000,000 are "poor,"—that is, are engaged in a grim and never-ceasing struggle for the bare necessities of life; and no fewer than 12,000,000 people are always, in the words of a British Prime Minister, "on the verge of starvation." Think of it: in that great and wealthy country, out of every seven persons six are so poor that it is a continual struggle for them to get enough food, fire, and clothing. In the slums of England's great cities there are millions of people housed as you or I would be ashamed to house a horse or a dog. In London alone, it has been calculated, there are more than a million persons who have to live upon sixpence a day. In 1909 there were, in Britain, 60,000 members of trades unions who could get no work to do—able-bodied men, trained to their work; and to these must be added many thousands of unskilled labourers. But perhaps the statement which shows most clearly of all what poverty has come to in Britain is this, that in a single year as much as £31,000,000 has been spent on relieving the poor by means of public charities; and, of course, we must add to this an immense amount—how much, we have no means of knowing—given privately by charitable persons. And the sad thing is that all this huge expenditure on charity, though it keeps people, for the moment, from dying of starvation, does nothing permanent towards abolishing poverty, or even diminishing the number of the poor; because it does nothing to remove the causes of poverty.

These figures show how absurd it is to think that because Australia is a rich country, great and widespread poverty is impossible here. The example of Britain shows that it is possible for a country which is exceedingly rich to have a vast mass of appallingly poor people in it. It all depends on the way in which the wealth is distributed; there may be vast wealth, but the benefits of that wealth may be enjoyed by a mere handful of the population. This is the case in Britain. It has been estimated that about one-seventieth part of the population owns far more than one half of the wealth of the United Kingdom. The British government at the present time is trying hard to find a cure for this desperate state of things. In Australia such a state of things has, happily, never come into existence, and it is the business of government to prevent it from ever coming into existence. Let us glance at some of the things which, among us, government does to prevent poverty, and also at what it does to relieve the poverty which already exists.

The prevention of poverty, like the prevention of disease, depends on a knowledge of causes. What are the causes of poverty? You will hear various answers given. Some people will tell you, for instance, that the poor have always themselves to blame; that they would not be poor if it were not for their own idleness, or wastefulness, or improvidence, or intemperance. Of the great majority of the poor this is absolutely untrue. These faults are *sometimes* the causes of poverty, but they are far more often the effects of it; and the majority of the poor are not idle or improvident or wasteful or intemperate. It may sound absurd, but it is true, that *the chief cause of poverty is poverty*. I mean, that poverty is a thing handed on from one generation to another; the reason why a man is poor is, in the majority of cases, that his parents were poor. It is the most difficult thing in the world to triumph over one's early surroundings. If a child's parents are desperately poor, if he is brought up amid squalid and wretched surroundings, if he is insufficiently fed, miserably clad, and housed in a mere den, the chances are that that child, when he becomes a man, will be as poor as his parents were. Not more than one in a thousand of the children of the poor could hope to escape from this tragic inheritance, if they were not helped. If government is going to prevent poverty, it must begin with the children, and help them to escape.

It does this, as we have seen, by means of education; and especially does it do this by means of technical education. The great majority of England's poor belong to the "unskilled labour" class; people who have not been trained to any special kind of work, who have no special skill at anything, and who therefore can do only the kind of work which requires no particular skill—like carrying heavy weights on a wharf or breaking stones on a road; and there are always far more men who can do this unskilled work than there is work for them to do. But the skilled craftsman can almost always—at least in Australia—find work to do, at wages at least sufficient to keep him from dire poverty. The aim of technical education is to teach young people to be skilful workers in various industries, and so to help them to earn a living. By providing a technical education, government enables the sons and daughters of the poorest to rise above the condition which their parents' poverty would otherwise have doomed them to.

In some cases it is necessary that children should be taken right away from the evil surroundings of their childhood, if they are to be saved from a life of poverty and even of crime, and become useful members of society. Much is done in all the states, both by private individuals and by government, to rescue the orphans and waifs, the neglected and destitute children, who are to be found in large numbers in every great city, and in country places also. These are sent to orphanages and industrial schools, where they are given food and shelter and are taught some trade or other. If a child has committed some offence, which shows that he is just beginning to slip into a life of crime, government does not send him to a prison, to herd with grown-up criminals and learn from them their vices, but to an industrial school or reformatory, where he acquires good habits and is shown how to earn an honest living. A good example of a reformatory was the Sobraon, a training ship for boys, provided by the New South Wales government. On this ship, five thousand boys have been trained, and it is said that out of every hundred of these, ninety-eight have turned out good citizens. (Perhaps the best illustration in the world of what can be done by taking children away from evil surroundings is to be found in England, in Dr. Barnardo's homes. This splendid institution has saved 70,000 children from the streets, and 98 per cent of these children have been made into decent and honest men and women.) In Australia, many of the reformatories are in private hands, but government pays them for the work they do, and exercises some supervision over them.

Another great cause of poverty is sickness; even a highly skilled workman may easily sink into a condition of poverty, not through any fault of his own, but through ill-health. So that government prevents poverty when it prevents disease; and we have already seen what efforts it makes for the prevention of disease. Here again, a great deal must be done with the children, and especially with the babies; for a strong and healthy babyhood is the only foundation for a strong and healthy manhood and womanhood. By ensuring to the poor a cheap and good milk-supply, and by giving ignorant mothers information about the proper feeding and management of babies, government can do a great deal for the health of the future nation. By providing good schoolrooms and good playgrounds, and by the medical inspection of schools, it does much for the health of the older children.

Again, there is no doubt that much poverty can be prevented by the practice of thrift. Everyone who possibly can should save money, so that when his "rainy day" comes, when accident or sickness or other misfortune lays its hand upon him, he may have enough laid by to tide him over his troubles without aid from others. Government cannot make people thrifty, but it can encourage habits of saving; and it does this by means of the Government Savings Banks, which are especially intended for the use of the poorer classes. The Savings Bank not only does not make us pay for its services, as the other banks do; it actually pays us interest on the money we put into it, and thus encourages us to leave our money in the bank as long as we possibly can.

In Germany, government encourages, or rather compels, thrift, and helps to prevent destitution, by means of a scheme of insurance against sickness. Both the workmen and their employers make weekly contributions to a fund, out of which assistance is given to those who suffer from sickness or disablement. Britain has lately followed the example of Germany in this matter; but under the British scheme, government makes a contribution to the fund, as well as the workman and his employer; and the workmen in certain trades are insured against unemployment, as well as against sickness and disablement. The contributions are made by means of a card, to which each week the workman affixes a stamp and his employer another. A stamp, of course, is simply a sign that you have paid a penny, or twopence, or whatever the value of the stamp may be, to government.

There are two other very important ways in which government strives to prevent poverty. First, by *industrial legislation*, which is an effort to secure to every worker, if not a fair reward for his labour, at least such a reward as will enable him to supply himself and his family with the necessities of life. And, secondly, by assisting in the production of wealth. But each of these matters is so important that it must have a chapter to itself.

CHAPTER XIII.

RELIEF OF POVERTY.

We have seen in the last chapter how government attacks some of the causes of poverty; how it tries to prevent poverty from occurring. But, in spite of all the efforts hitherto made, poverty does occur; no government in the world has yet succeeded in preventing it. Even in this favoured land of ours, there is poverty on every side of us; not so widespread, it is true, and not of such terrible intensity, as in many of the older countries; but still widespread enough and terrible enough. What is the attitude of government towards the poor? Does it leave them to battle with circumstances as best they can, or does it make any attempt to relieve their distress? You know the answer: in every modern civilized nation it is thought that government has a duty to perform towards the poor. It is accepted as a rule, that no member of society must be allowed to die for lack of food, of warmth, or of medical aid; if private charity fails, government must step in to prevent this from happening. Unhappily, people do die of starvation, even in civilized countries; in England, every year (in spite of the many millions of pounds spent every year on the relief of poverty), some deaths do occur, to which the doctors can assign no other cause but lack of sufficient nourishment. But whenever this happens, it is felt to be a disgrace to a civilized nation.

This is another illustration of the fact, already mentioned, that in modern times government does far more,—touches people's lives at a far greater number of points,—than it did in ancient times. *Private* efforts to help the poor are, of course, by no means a new thing; in one of the most ancient books in the world we may read of a rich man who prided himself on being "a father to the poor," and of the duty of assisting "the widow and the fatherless." In the middle ages we find a great advance on private charity,—namely, public institutions, such as asylums and hospitals; but these were built and managed, not by government, but by the Christian Church, and were supported by gifts to the church. It is only in modern times that we find government taking poverty seriously in hand, and accepting the relief of distress as one of its duties. It is only in modern times that this general principle has been accepted: that if any member of the community cannot provide for himself, he must be provided for by the community.

Roughly speaking, we may say that the community—by means of its machinery of government,—helps six different classes of poor people. (1) The children of the poor; (2) those who are unable to work because of sickness; (3) those who are unable to work because of some defect of body or mind, such as the blind, the deaf-and-dumb, the insane, and persons of defective intellect; (4) those who are unable to work because of old age; (5) the unemployed; and (6) paupers.

Enough has already been said about the various ways in which government helps poor children; enough, too, about the hospitals and asylums for the sick and for those suffering from some bodily or mental defect. For the second and third classes, however, something more is required than hospitals and asylums can give. The hospital gives the best medical treatment to a sick man, but it can do nothing to relieve the distress of the wife and children who are dependent on his weekly earnings for their livelihood. Moreover, ill-health may prevent a man from working, without his being sufficiently sick to be given a bed in a hospital. What is to become of him, and of his family? He may receive aid, not from society as a whole, but from a smaller society of which he is a member. If he is a wise man, and has been able to afford it, he has paid something every week while he was in good health to the funds of a *friendly society* of some kind; and now that he is sick, that society comes to his aid, granting him *sick* pay which partly makes up for the loss of his earnings. If, however, he is too poor to belong to a friendly society, he will have to turn for aid to some private charitable institution. But here, also, government is beginning to step in; the parliament of the Commonwealth has passed a law, whereby government may provide an *invalid pension* to anyone above the age of sixteen suffering from permanent disablement or ill-health.

The modern belief, we have seen, is that society must help the helpless; and this has led, in recent times, to a great deal of attention being given to the aged poor; for the very old are often as helpless as the very young. Until quite lately, the chief way in which society helped old men and women no longer able to earn a living was to bring them into some public institution,—Benevolent Asylums, Homes for the Destitute, and so forth. There are many such institutions in Australia; they are carried on partly by government aid, partly by public subscription, partly by private gifts, and partly by small payments made by the relatives of the old people who are fed and sheltered in them. But this is not altogether satisfactory; it was long felt that the old ought to be helped without being taken away from their own homes and their own families. In 1898 the government of New Zealand introduced a system of *Old-age Pensions*. The example of New Zealand was quickly followed by Victoria, New South Wales, and Queensland; finally, in 1908, the Commonwealth took the matter over from the states, and provided for the payment of old-age pensions all over Australia. The pension is paid to all *men* requiring it who are sixty-five years old, or, if they are permanently unable to work, sixty years old; and to all *women* requiring it who are sixty years old. The amount of the pension is fixed in each case by the Commissioner of Pensions, or by one of his assistants; but it must not in any case be more than ten shillings per week. This may seem a small amount, but remember that the system as a whole is a very costly business,—so costly that for a long time many people thought that it was an impossible scheme, and that the community would not be able to bear the expense.

By the unemployed, we mean those who are willing to work, and who are not debarred from working by sickness or any other cause, but who cannot find work to do. Government may assist these unfortunates in several ways. First, it may *employ* them,—for of course government, with all the public work it has to do, is a large employer of labour; it may set them to work at road-making, or railway construction, or the digging of irrigation channels, or any other piece of work which they are fit for and which government wants done. Secondly, by means of the *government labour bureau*, it can put these men who want work in touch with private employers who want workers; and when a man has obtained work in the country, but cannot get to it because he cannot pay his railway fare, the bureau lends him the necessary money. Thirdly, by means of such institutions as the Labour Colony at Leongatha, in Victoria, government gives temporary assistance to able-bodied men who are willing to work. At this place men are taught how to work on a farm, and are paid wages for the work they do while they are there; as soon as they have earned a little money they must leave in search of work elsewhere, but this temporary relief has saved many a man from starving.

Lastly, we come to the paupers. You may have thought that "pauper" was just another name for "poor man," but it is not so. Pauperism is far worse than poverty; I may be a very poor man without becoming a pauper. Happily for us, there is not, and we may hope there will never be, a permanent pauper class in Australia; and so we are saved from a dark problem which the government of every country in Europe has to face,—the problem of pauperism;

the question of how to deal with multitudes of idle and shiftless persons who, from lack of physical energy, stamina, will-power, and brain-power, cannot earn their own living for a week. In Great Britain it is calculated that thirty-eight persons out of every thousand are paupers—persons who cannot keep themselves, and for whose sustenance the whole country has to be taxed. This is the real problem of poor-relief; by simply giving a man money and food we tend to make him a pauper, and so to rob him of all self-respect; for one who cannot earn his own living, but lives at the expense of others, is very likely to lose self-respect, and the many good qualities that are founded on self-respect. (It is true that many very rich men resemble paupers in this, that they live, not by their own exertions, but by the toil of others. These, too, one would think, must lose all self-respect; certainly they can have no claim to other people's respect.) In other countries, paupers are dealt with by workhouses, poorhouses, almshouses, and other means. In Australia, as I have said, we have practically no pauperism; for though we may sometimes have among us a considerable number of unemployed, we are not burdened with those unfortunate beings known in Britain as "unemployables."

CHAPTER XIV.

PRODUCTION OF WEALTH.

There is another way in which government can prevent poverty, and that is by assisting people in the production of wealth. What we call material wealth is got, directly or indirectly, from the land. There are two ways in which men create wealth: first, by working on the land, and producing what we call raw material, such as corn, or wool, or iron; secondly, by working up these raw materials into manufactured articles,—making the corn into bread, the wool into clothing, the iron into machines. Government assists in the production both of raw material and of manufactured articles; assists in so many ways that to give a mere list of them would fill this chapter. We must choose some one example: let us look at the way in which government helps the *farmers*, the men who are producing some of the most absolutely necessary of all raw materials.

Government helps the farmers, in the first place, by research,—the pursuit of scientific knowledge. Farming is not a thing that stands still; new knowledge is constantly being brought to bear on it; new and better methods are constantly displacing the old; and the men who adopt the new methods are the men who succeed. Now the search for new knowledge of this kind can only be carried on, at least in new countries like ours, by government; it is a long and costly business, and could not be undertaken by individual farmers. Farming is not carried on, like mining, by rich companies, but by separate individuals, each with his own small block of land;

and, for the most part, it is not a business which brings men great fortunes, though it provides a comfortable living to the industrious. The farmer, therefore, cannot afford the time, nor has he the training, to seek for new methods of production. He learns a great deal by practice, but in the growing of plants and the rearing of animals there is much that cannot be learnt by practice, but only by scientific research and experiment. The farmer, working hard on his farm, could not be expected to find out for himself what was the best and cheapest cure for fungoid diseases on his fruit trees, the best way of preventing tuberculosis in his cattle, or the best form in which to supply phosphates as a food for his crops. In that branch of government which is called the Department of Agriculture, in each of the Australian States, research of this kind is always going on; chemists are constantly studying the nature of the soil and seeking for the proper manures to enrich it; botanists are studying the conditions of the healthy life and growth of plants; bacteriologists and entomologists study the various diseases and insect foes from which plants and animals suffer. Then, too, government carries on *experimental farms*, where experiments are conducted which show what crops are best suited to the soil and climate, what are the best manures for each particular crop, and so on. The officers of government also keep in touch with the similar work that is being done by other governments, so that when a discovery important to farmers is made in any part of the world, it is quickly known in Australia. All this complicated and expensive work could not possibly be carried on by individual farmers; yet, for the sake of the general prosperity of the country, it must be done by some one. Only government can do it.

The knowledge thus gained must be communicated to the farmers and applied by them. In the first place, government provides, as we have seen, agricultural high schools and agricultural colleges, where boys are taught the best and newest methods in every branch of farming. In the second place, government sends round experts to give instructions to the farmers; and it publishes pamphlets and magazines which are put into the hands of every farmer who is sensible enough to want to read them. In every possible way it tries to spread a knowledge of the latest discoveries and the best methods.

Both plants and animals are liable to diseases of various kinds; and without assistance from government, farmers could not hold their own in the incessant warfare which must be waged against these diseases. In the first place, government does what no individual farmer could possibly do,—it guards the ports, and prevents diseased animals, plants, or fruits, from being brought into the country. For instance, the government of Victoria has arranged for a careful examination of all fruit coming from New South Wales, Queensland, and elsewhere, in order to prevent the *fruit-fly* from coming into Victoria. This examination protects the fruit-growers from an insect which, if it once got a footing in Victoria, would certainly ruin many of them. Perhaps in no country in the world are horses, cattle, and sheep so free from disease as they are in Australia; and this is partly due to the unwinking watch kept by government to prevent the importation of diseased stock.

But the vigilance of government does not end at the ports. It takes measures also to prevent the spread of pests and diseases whenever they appear; and here again government does what the farmers could not do for themselves, just because it has the power of making laws, and of enforcing them. A farmer, for instance, might allow a noxious weed to grow unchecked in his paddocks, a weed whose seeds would presently be blown all over the district; and so by his carelessness he would injure, not only himself, but his neighbours. Government can do what his neighbours cannot do: it can insist on his destroying the weed. Government inspectors travel round the country continually to see that everyone is obeying the law by keeping rabbits in check; other inspectors visit orchards to see that fruit trees are sprayed and kept free from various pests; and so on.

When an infectious disease has broken out among the cattle of a particular locality, that locality is declared an "infected area," and no cattle are allowed to pass beyond its boundaries until the disease is stamped out. In ways such as these, government uses the force of law to protect the farmers.

Then, again, in this country large tracts of land would be unfit for agriculture, because of the insufficient rainfall, if it were not for irrigation, which makes use of those great volumes of water which would otherwise flow away into the sea and be wasted. Government has spent enormous sums on irrigation, and will spend much more in the future, making rich and productive land out of what would otherwise be barren desert. The farmers, working by themselves, could no more provide these dams and channels to water their land than they could provide railways to carry their goods to market. Making the railway freights as cheap as possible is another way in which government can encourage agriculture; and yet another way is by seeing that cheap land is available for everyone who wishes to go in for farming. To get a supply of land for this purpose, government has sometimes to buy from their owners large estates, and cut them up into smaller blocks suitable for farms. In short, the idea now prevails that it is the duty of government to assist and encourage farming in every possible way.

It should be pointed out, however, that even when a farmer is not helped by Government, he is greatly helped by being a member of society; that is, he is helped by, and helps, his neighbours. What individual farmers, working separately, could never do—that may be done by a group of farmers working together, or "co-operating" as it is called. When, for instance, a group of dairy farmers unite to build a creamery or a butter-factory, where the milk of each of their separate farms is treated, they are enabled to get a reward from their labours far greater than any they could have got if they had not united.

BEREMBED WEIR, N.S.W.

The dairy farmers of Australia have long since found out this secret of co-operation, and the fruit-growers are beginning to find it out.

The help given to farmers is only one example of the way in which government assists the production of wealth; many other examples might have been chosen. I might have told you, for instance, about the work done by the Mines Department, and about the great sums of money that have been spent by the various Australian governments on the encouragement of mining. And government assistance by no means stops at the production of raw material; the assistance and encouragement of *manufactures* has been regarded as a duty of government almost since the beginning of Australian history. The chief way in which government has assisted manufacturers is by imposing customs duties,—taxes on manufactured articles brought in from abroad. But this, with other taxes, will be spoken of in a later chapter.

CHAPTER XV.

COMMUNICATIONS

(a) The Post Office.

The chief business of the Post Office is the conveyance of letters and newspapers; but several other matters are, in Australia, dealt with by this great department of government. It controls the electric telegraph system; the telephones, also, are under its management; it looks after the conveyance of parcels and packets; and the money order office is one of its branches. If you wish to send a letter to a friend at a distance, or to telegraph to him, or to speak to him on the telephone, or to send him a book, or to send him a sum of money, you can do all these things quickly, cheaply, and safely by means of the Post Office. The management of this vast system of communication was, as we have noted, one of the tasks taken over from the separate States of Australia by the Commonwealth. At the head of it all is the Postmaster-General, who is a member of the Commonwealth cabinet. Under his command is a great army of officials, postmasters, clerks, letter-sorters, letter-carriers, telegraph-boys, telephone-operators, engineers, mechanics, labourers, and so on.

Some sort of postal system existed in very ancient times; in fact, it is not easy to see how the government of any large country could ever have been carried on, if the central governing body had had no means of sending messages to, and getting news from, distant parts of the country. But, until comparatively recent times, if you

LETTER SORTING IN AN AUSTRALIAN POST OFFICE

wanted to send a letter to a friend, you had to engage a messenger to take it, either running on foot or, if horses were available, riding on horseback. These messengers were called "posts,"—which is the origin of the expression "post-haste," since these messengers were in a greater hurry than ordinary travellers. Needless to say, the sending of letters was a slow and a costly business in those days; and private persons could rarely afford to write to one another, especially if they were far apart. The system of mail-coaches, which was introduced into England towards the close of the eighteenth century, was a great improvement; but even then the sending of letters was so expensive, that it may safely be said that the great majority, even of those who could read and write, passed their whole lives without receiving or sending a single letter. Then came the railway; and, ten years later, Rowland Hill with his two great reforms—the penny post, and the adhesive postage stamp. Rowland Hill was the real founder of the modern post-office; his invention, as Gladstone said, "ran like a wildfire through the civilized world." Every civilized country in the world has now a postal system, and uses postage stamps.

In Australia, there was a post office, of a somewhat primitive kind, a good many years before Rowland Hill's reforms had been heard of. "The first Australian office for postal purposes was established in Sydney by Lieutenant-Governor Paterson under a Government order dated the 25th April, 1809, which declared that owing to complaints having been made that numerous frauds had been committed by individuals repairing on board ships on their arrival in port, and personating others, by which they wrongfully obtained possession of letters and parcels, the Lieutenant-Governor had established an office at which all parcels and letters arriving by any vessel, addressed to the inhabitants of the colony, were to be deposited previous to their distribution. The office was in High Street (now known as George Street) at the residence of Mr. Isaac Nicholls, who was empowered 'in consideration of the trouble and expense attendant on this duty,' to charge on delivery to the addressee the following sums:—For every letter, one shilling; for every parcel not exceeding 20 lbs. weight, two shillings and sixpence; and for all exceeding that weight, five shillings. A list was to be published in the *Gazette* of the names of persons to whom letters and parcels were directed.'" Such was the crude beginning, a century ago, of our postal system. Think of what it has grown to since then!

There are now more than 5,000 post-offices in the Commonwealth; there is no township in Australia, however insignificant and however remote, that has not its own post-office, from which people can send letters to any part of the civilized world. More than 24,000 persons are employed in the service of the Postmaster-General's department. There are 94,000 miles of telegraph wire in use in the Commonwealth; and over 145,000 miles of telephone wire. The Department pays about a quarter of a million pounds sterling every year as subsidies to various lines of steamers, which convey our letters to and from Europe, Asia, Africa, America, and the Islands of the Pacific; besides large subsidies to the companies which own submarine cables. These facts and figures may help you to realise the enormous growth of our postal system since the days when Mr. Isaac Nicholls distributed the Australian mails from his house in High Street, Sydney.

But there are some other figures which ought to bring the contrast more vividly before our minds. Every country which is civilized enough to have a post-office has learnt Rowland Hill's lesson—that it pays best to carry letters as cheaply as possible. Before Hill's reforms were introduced, it cost, in England, fourpence to send a letter ten miles; it can now be sent ten thousand miles for a penny! A Londoner had to pay 1s. 4½d. to send a letter to Edinburgh; for a penny he can now send a letter to Sydney. We in Australia can for a penny

7   Commonwealth Year-Book, No. 1, p. 599.

send a letter, not merely to any place in the Commonwealth, but to any place in the British Empire; and twopence-halfpenny will take a letter to any foreign country. This cheapening of the postal rates has resulted in an enormous expansion of the business done by the Post Office. In one year, the Australian Post Office carries more than three hundred and fifty millions of letters and postcards; besides a hundred millions of newspapers! In one year, more than ten millions of letters and postcards are sent from Australia to other countries. The figures are so big that it is difficult to grasp their meaning.

The service rendered to us by the Post Office is a thing to which we have been accustomed all our lives, and for that reason we seldom consider how wonderful it really is. When you carelessly drop into a box a letter addressed to a friend in London, with the utmost confidence that, a month hence, a postman will step up to your friend's door and deliver your letter, do you ever reflect on the triumph of management implied in this? When your letter is once in the box, with a penny stamp on it as a sign that you have paid a penny to the Government, the Post Office takes care of it, protects it from accidents and from thieves, hurries it to a railway train, hurries it across the sea, sends it from Italy to England as fast as an express train and a turbine steamer can carry it, never ceases to look after it until it has been put into your friend's hands; and all this for a penny.

The Post Office does all this with every letter and newspaper and packet entrusted to its care, by means of an elaborate system, which has been brought to its present state of excellence after years of effort, and to the perfecting of which many men have devoted their lives. And remember that this system, to be effective, has to be world-wide. The Governments of the various countries do not act together about many matters; but they act together about this. Australia is a member of what is called the Universal Postal Union, which holds a conference from time to time, to which all the principal governments of the world send representatives; in this way the different nations are constantly finding improved methods of carrying one another's letters. The Post Office has rendered an enormous service to civilization. One of the great obstacles to civilization has always been *space*,—the distance between one town and another, the distance between one country and another. When we make communication cheap, and quick, and easy, we rob space of its terrors; we bring the population of the whole world closer together; we *destroy* space. Not so very many years ago, it took three months for a letter to go from Sydney to London; it now takes about a month; may we not say, then, that in a very real sense Sydney has been brought nearer to London? But if a month is too long a time, if your business is urgent and you require an immediate answer, you can send a cablegram to London and have a reply in a few hours. Man has harnessed the lightning to serve his needs, and bidden it carry his messages along the floor of the sea; and that has meant a triumph over space. The invention that has brought us nearest to the absolute annihilation of space is the telephone, which enables you, sitting in a room in Melbourne, to talk to a man in Sydney as if he were in the same room with you. Some day perhaps you will be able to talk, in the same way, to a man in London, or in New York, or in St. Petersburg; if that day ever comes, then indeed our victory over space will be complete, so far as communication is concerned.

The Post Office is a great public educator. When letters, books, and newspapers can be easily and cheaply sent to and from all parts of the country, nobody, in however remote a township he may live, is cut off from the stream of ideas. It enables us to know what other people are thinking and talking about; and in this way it not only prevents ignorance, but it also prevents isolation; it knits the whole people more firmly together, and helps to make national life possible—to keep alive in us the sense of being united to our fellow-countrymen. Finally, the Post Office is the great servant of trade and commerce. The vast and intricate structure of modern commerce

A TELEPHONE EXCHANGE.

would fall to the ground at once if the postal and telegraphic systems were destroyed. For nowadays commerce is not conducted by men going down into the market-place and bargaining with one another by word of mouth. A merchant in a London office dictates a telegram, and a few hours later money changes hands in Pekin. A piece of news appears in the morning papers in Berlin, and a few hours later the price of wheat has risen in the United States. The whole commercial world is held together by a network of telegraph wires.

But we must be careful not to think of the Post Office as merely the servant of those engaged in trade; it is the servant of every one of us, great and small. Even if you never send and never receive a letter or a telegram, you are still heavily indebted to the Post Office; for you live in the midst of, and enjoy whatever is good in, a civilization which would certainly not be what it is had it not been for the work of this great department of government. The postal system is one of the most important ways in which government has helped, and is helping, society.

CHAPTER XVI.

COMMUNICATIONS.

(b) RAILWAYS.

As we have already noticed, road-making has been, from very early times, one of the important tasks of government; and in the number and quality of the roads in any country we find a sure sign of the degree of civilization which that country has reached. But in a new country like ours, a country of vast spaces and possessing very few navigable rivers, the iron road is the most important of all roads. And all the Australian states seem to have recognised its importance; for they have spent, between them, not far short of one-hundred-and-fifty millions of pounds on the work of making and equipping railways. This is a huge sum; was government really justified in spending so much of the people's money on this one thing? To answer that question, we shall have to ask another,—Why are railways important?

In the first place, we have seen how great a part is played, among all civilized peoples, by the post office; and the railway is the trusty servant of the post office. We have seen that the post office aims at robbing distance of its terrors, by means of rapidity in the carrying of our messages to one another; this rapidity it achieves partly by the use of electricity; but mainly, and so far as the great mass of our correspondence is concerned, by the use of steam-power. Think how slow and expensive it would be, if all letters from Brisbane to Adelaide had to be carried in coaches drawn by horses! If the railways carried letters and nothing else, they would still be among the greatest of our servants.

But, in the second place, they carry persons. If you look at a railway map of Australia, you will see that only a narrow fringe of our great continent is as yet supplied with railways; but already some long journeys are possible. For instance, you can travel by train from Longreach, in the middle of Queensland, by way of Brisbane, Sydney, Melbourne, and Adelaide, to Oodnadatta, in the middle of South Australia—a distance of 3,300 miles. You can go by train from Brisbane to Adelaide in three days; and before very long you will be able to travel, in one unbroken railway journey, from Rockhampton in Queensland to Geraldton in Western Australia. There will still be vast tracts of country which you will be able to reach only by means of horses or camels; it will be many years—perhaps centuries—before a network of railways is spread over the whole continent. But meanwhile, on the 16,000 miles of railway which we already possess, think of the crowds of people constantly moving to and fro, on business or pleasure! The whole population seems to be moving, to a degree undreamed of in any country of the world a hundred years ago. And one advantage of this, apart altogether from the great advantage to trade, is that it has helped the growth of a national Australian feeling; people are constantly moving from one state to another, and thus the people of the different states have got to know one another, and to feel that they are one nation.

But perhaps the advantage of being able to travel by rail is most keenly felt in the neighbourhood of a great city. Men and women whose daily work is in the city are not forced to live in the city, crowded together in an unhealthy way, in order to be near their work; they can live at some distance from the city, in healthy suburbs where every house has a garden round it, and be carried rapidly and cheaply to and from their work by means of the railways. In Melbourne thousands of people use the suburban trains every morning and evening; in Sydney the same work is done by electric trams—and a tramway is just a railway in the middle of a street. In London, the railway has been an unspeakable gain to the working population; a vast network of lines—many of them laid in tunnels deep under the ground—has gone far to solve the terrible problem of overcrowding.

But, after all, perhaps the most useful function of the railway is the carrying, not of letters nor of persons, but of goods. Its importance as the carrier of goods is twofold. Take one example—the farmer. We have seen that government helps him in many ways,—finding out for him the latest methods of production, helping him to fight pests and disease, helping him to water his crops, and so on. Well, but it would not be of much use helping the farmer to produce if he could not dispose of his products. In the farming business, how to produce is only half the problem; the other half is, how to find a market for your products. No farmer can succeed unless he has some way of conveying his products cheaply and quickly to some place where they are wanted, where there are buyers for them. It would be of no use to tell a farmer about a wonderfully fertile piece of land in the centre of Australia, where he could grow marvellous crops of wheat; you might irrigate this piece of land for him, and show him how to protect his wheat from rust, and give him seed free of charge,—it would all be of no avail, because, having produced his wheat, he would not know what to do with it; he would not be able to get it carried, except at ruinous cost, from the farm to the buyer.

First, then, railways serve us by carrying the things we produce to the place where they are wanted, or to a sea-port from which they can be sent across the sea to the place where they are wanted. And, secondly, they serve us by carrying to us the things that other people produce; they bring to our doors the products of other districts, other states, other continents.

Do you realise what a service to civilization has been wrought by the men who have taught steam to carry our goods for us? Not so

CENTRAL RAILWAY STATION, MELBOURNE.

very long ago, great numbers of people might die of famine while, a few hundred miles away, crops lay rotting on the ground; there was abundance of food, but no means of carrying it to where men and women were perishing for lack of it. Not long ago, poor people were limited to the kinds of food produced in their locality; the labourer counted himself very well off if he could get enough of the few foods produced in his own immediate neighbourhood. Now, all is changed; look in the grocer's window, and you will see that even the poor man's table may draw upon the resources of the whole world. The Tasmanian can eat bananas brought from Queensland, the Queenslander can eat Tasmanian apples; the Londoner can have pineapples from Fiji; sugar, which years ago was a luxury only to be indulged in sparingly even by the rich, is now freely used by all but the destitute. This change is mainly due to the new means of transportation by sea and land; and if you think for a little you will see that railways have played a far more important part in the improvement than steamships. Sailing vessels might do all that is required in the way of carrying goods by sea, but for the cheap and rapid carrying of goods between sea-ports and inland towns, the coming of steam was necessary.

Of course I do not mean that a varied dinner-table is the foundation of civilization; food is only one example out of many which might have been given; we might have taken wool, or cotton, or iron, or manufactured articles. The rapid distribution of goods, which has been made possible by the invention of the locomotive, has changed the lives of all of us. It has cheapened the necessaries of life; it has made many things accessible to the poor which were formerly accessible only to the rich; and it has made us regard as necessaries things that were formerly regarded as luxuries.

There is another point of view from which we can see the importance of railways: the point of view of Defence. If Australia were invaded by a foreign foe, it would be all-important for our commander-in-chief to be able to move large bodies of soldiers, with the utmost possible speed, to the point where they were wanted. In the old days, when troops could only get from place to place by marching along the roads, getting an army together when it was wanted was a slow business; but the railway has revolutionized warfare. So long as our railways were not destroyed by the enemy, we could concentrate the military strength of Australia wherever it might be required, instead of having an army scattered over the Commonwealth, and therefore useless. Moreover, when you have got an army together, you have to feed it; by means of the railway we could carry supplies of food to our soldiers wherever they might be.

Finally, the railway is the great instrument for "opening up" a new country. In the early days of Australian history, people settled down in the sea-ports, or close to them; only the more adventurous spirits went far inland, and we cannot wonder at this, for to go inland meant to be cut off from the comforts of civilization, and from communication with one's fellow-men. To induce people to settle in the interior, it was necessary to make the interior fit for human habitation. When a railway is carried inland, population soon follows; because people know that, when they have a railway near them, they have a means of getting their goods to market; a means of obtaining the goods they need; and a means of getting away, if need be.

In Australia, practically all the railway lines are owned and managed by government. Why is this? Why could the railways not have been left, as they are left in Great Britain, to private companies? One reason is that Great Britain is an old and populous country, and Australia a new and thinly populated country. To open up and develop our country, it was necessary to build railways, even though there was no prospect of making a profit out of them for years to come. Making a railway is a very costly affair. The railways of Australia, on an average, have cost £9,500 per *mile* to construct. No

GOING HOME FROM THE CITY

private company can be expected to invest huge sums of money in an undertaking which will bring no profit for many years, and which may never bring a profit—except, of course, the profit it brings to the community generally. For the sake of getting the country populated, it was necessary to build railways; no private company would do it; therefore, it was necessary for government to do it.

There is another reason why, in a new country, it is thought best for government to own the railways. In Britain, if one company charges you too much for carrying your goods from London to Edinburgh, you can send them by another company's line; the competition of many companies keeps prices down. But nothing like this could have happened in Australia. If a private company had been willing to risk an enormous sum of money in constructing a railway, say, from Melbourne to Mildura, it would have done so only if it had been promised a *monopoly*; that is, if it had been promised that government would allow no other company to take away half its profits by building another line from Melbourne to Mildura. And, having a monopoly, that company would have made its fares and freights as high as possible; it would have charged as much as it could induce people to pay for carrying themselves and their goods. For the sake of the development of the country, it was necessary, not only that goods should be carried rapidly, but that they should be carried cheaply. So that even if private companies had been willing to build our railways, it would still have been best, for the sake of cheapness, that they should be built by government.

CHAPTER XVII.

INDUSTRIAL LEGISLATION

During the closing years of the eighteenth century and the opening years of the nineteenth, Britain, which had hitherto been mainly an agricultural country, became mainly a manufacturing country. The causes of this "industrial revolution," as it is called—a revolution of far-reaching importance, which changed the whole life of the nation—were many; but the chief cause was a series of wonderful inventions, which introduced *machinery* into one industry after another. The result was the factory system—the growth of great manufacturing cities, the enormous increase of population in those cities, the transference of population from country to town. For many a year, Britain had no serious rival, either in the manufacture of goods or in the carrying of those goods to all parts of the world; Britain became the manufacturer and the carrier for the whole world. The consequence of this preeminence was, that Britain became immensely wealthy; her factory-owners and her merchants heaped up for themselves enormous fortunes. The spectacle of all this growing wealth and prosperity is doubtless a pleasing one, but if we look behind the outward show we shall see something not quite so pleasant; we shall see on the one hand unscrupulous greed and merciless cruelty, and on the other hand poverty and misery and degradation the like of which the country had never known before in all the centuries of its history. Everywhere we shall see the factory-owner clamouring for cheap labour—and getting it; we shall see him using men, women, and children as means of filling his purse, and treating them with far less regard for their welfare than if they were horses or dogs. The nineteenth century, it has been said, will be known in the history of Britain as "the wicked century." And if we are inclined to think that that is an exaggeration, let us look at the treatment of children, in factories and elsewhere, during that century.

The cry was for cheap labour—and what labour could be cheaper than the labour of little children, who could be "apprenticed" to factory-owners, and made to work without wages till they reached manhood or womanhood? Thousands of children were sent to the manufacturing cities and handed over to the tender mercies of the factory-owners—practically sold into slavery; there is one instance of a gang of little children being actually sold as part of a bankrupt's property. Children as young as three-and-a-half were made to work long hours in the most unhealthy conditions; quite young children had to work as much as eighteen hours a day! In the cotton mills, many children worked all night; and it was a common thing to keep children of six years old at work from six in the morning till seven at night. In the brick fields, so late as 1871, there were thirty thousand children at work, mostly girls, many of them only four years old. Naturally, children who worked for so many hours a day in unventilated factories, badly fed and utterly uncared-for, died like flies; and those of them who did contrive to grow up were ruined in health, and became weak, stunted, and miserable men and women. Worst off of all, perhaps, were the children condemned to work in mines. About the middle of the century Lord Shaftesbury persuaded Parliament to appoint a committee to enquire into child labour in mines. That committee issued a report, which is one of the most terrible documents in existence. It told of little children of three and four working in the dark and damp of the mine all day long, and never seeing the daylight except on Sundays. It told of young girls whose business it was to drag trucks of coal along the narrow tunnels; they had to crawl on all fours, with a chain hooked on to the trucks and to belts round their waists. And this took place, remember, in the nineteenth century, in the midst of a nation calling itself civilized and Christian; a nation which professed to worship that lover of little children who spoke the stern and terrible words,—"Whosoever shall offend against one of these little ones, it were better for him that a mill-stone were hanged about his neck, and that he were drowned in the depth of the sea."

But, however factory-owners might forget everything else in their inhuman lust for wealth, the British nation was still sound at heart; and when the facts were made known, and the nation's conscience was at last awakened, steps were taken to put an end to all this cruelty. This is not a history of England, and I need not describe the various "factory acts" by which the load was gradually lifted from the children's shoulders.

But it will be useful to ask ourselves, why these factory laws came so slowly and were met by so much opposition; why a kindly and humane people for so many years put up with a state of things so hideous? The answer is, that great numbers of people in Britain in the nineteenth century were under the sway of two very false ideas. The first was, that if a father liked to send a child away, at four years of age, to be overworked in a factory, government must not interfere, because a father is free to do what he likes with his own child; it would be an interference with "parental rights." They forgot that a child has rights too, and that a parent has duties as well as rights,—duties which it may be necessary to compel him to perform. The second idea was that a factory-owner must be allowed to manage his factory as he pleased, that government must never interfere between an employer and those he employs, that all such interference is an interference with liberty. They forgot that the children's liberty was also of importance; and that the factory-owner's liberty meant the children's slavery. If you ever hear people saying that the state ought

A COOKERY CLASS.

not to interfere in matters of industry, remember the British coal-mines and cotton-mills of the early nineteenth century; and think of all that state interference has meant for hundreds of thousands of children.

In Australia, at any rate, government does interfere with industries; and not on behalf of children only, but on behalf of all employees; especially those employed in shops and mines and factories. It is not necessary to describe what has been done, in this matter, in each of the states separately; let us confine our attention to Victoria, which had the honour of leading the way for the other states (by the Factories Act of 1873), and which still has the completest set of laws relating to industrial matters. ("Industrial matters" may be roughly defined as matters pertaining to the relations of employers and employees.)

The aims of these industrial laws are—to prevent working people from being paid unreasonably low wages, to prevent them from having to work for unreasonably long hours, to prevent them from having to work in unhealthy conditions, and, generally, to improve the lot of the labourers and protect them against injustice and greed. But here a word of caution is necessary; you must not for a moment suppose that employers as a class are unjust and greedy, or that these laws simply aim at protecting the employee against his employer. They protect the employer also; they protect, that is, the good employer, who pays fair wages and treats his employees well, against the competition of the bad employer, who pays the lowest wages he can, and treats his employees badly. If it were not for industrial laws, the bad employer, who can produce his goods more cheaply than the man who pays fair wages, would be able to undersell the latter and perhaps to ruin him.

As to the fixing of wages, this is so important a matter that it must be dealt with in a separate chapter. Let us now look at the other matters touched by industrial laws in Victoria.

First, as to factories. (A factory is defined, in Victorian law, as a place where four or more persons are employed in making or preparing articles for trade or sale, or any place where steam or other mechanical power is used in the preparation of such articles.) Government inspectors have the power to enter a factory at any reasonable hour of day or night, to inspect it thoroughly, and to ask questions of any person employed in it. Every factory must be kept clean, wholesome, and well-ventilated; must be thoroughly cleansed at regular intervals; and must be provided with a proper supply of fresh drinking water. Fire escapes must be provided, and proper appliances for extinguishing fires. (Only the other day, at a great fire in New York, a number of girls lost their lives simply because there were no fire escapes in the factory in which they were employed.) Precautions must be taken to prevent persons suffering from an infectious disease working in the factory. All dangerous machinery, vats, and anything else that is dangerous, must be properly fenced in. Persons in charge of engines or boilers must hold certificates showing that they have been trained and are competent for the work. Women and children must not be employed in the working of dangerous machinery; nor in cleaning any machinery while it is in motion. There are special rules for dangerous trades; for instance, no boys or girls under eighteen must be employed in the work of match-dipping, or silvering mirrors, or manufacturing white lead. No boy under fourteen or girl under fifteen years of age must be employed. No employee in a factory must be paid less than 2s. 6d. per week. (This, of course, is only meant as a protection for the youngest workers.)

For women, girls, and boys under sixteen the hours of employment are strictly limited; they must not work more than forty-eight hours per week, and they must not work more than ten hours in one day. No women or girls must be employed after the hour of nine in the evening. As to the hours of work for grown-up men, the

Victorian factory laws say nothing; because the men have (by means of their trades-unions, to be spoken of in the next chapter,) already secured the *eight-hours' system.*

As for shops: the hours in which they may be kept open for business are limited by law. In Victoria, shops are required to close at 6 p.m. on four days of the week; at 10 p.m. on one day; and at 1 p.m. on Saturday, which is a general half-holiday. No-one must be employed for more than fifty-two hours per week. Some kinds of shops—such as hotels and restaurants, chemists' and tobacconists' shops, and a few others—are treated as exceptions to these rules; but for them, too, the hours of closing are regulated by law. Various other rules have been made for the protection of shop assistants; as, for instance, the rule that chairs must be provided for saleswomen.

As for mines, there are laws for them also. Women, and boys under fourteen, are not allowed to be employed underground; and there are certain kinds of work on which no boy under seventeen must be employed. Various precautions must be taken to protect the miners from ill-health and from accidents; and injured miners, or the relatives of miners who have been killed, are enabled to get compensation from the mine-owners if the injury or death has been due to neglect of these precautions.

The hours of labour are limited, as in factories and shops; Sunday labour is forbidden; and so on. This is far from being a complete account of the laws relating to factories, shops, and mines; but I have told you some of the main provisions—enough, at any rate, to enable you to understand something of the way in which, in Australia, government interferes in industrial matters in order to protect the lives, the health, and the happiness of men, women, and children.

CHAPTER XVIII.

REGULATION OF WAGES.

The modern trade unions are the successors of the *craft guilds* which flourished, in England and elsewhere, during the Middle Ages; these, in their turn, may have been the successors of workers' unions among the Greeks and Romans; we even read of a kind of trade union in the Bible. But there is no room, in this little book, for ancient history; the trade union as we know it began somewhere in the early years of the nineteenth century. We have seen how the factory system brought misery to the child workers; but it brought misery to grown-up workers too; and the men soon began to do what children were helpless to attempt: they began to fight for better conditions. But they saw that in order to fight to any purpose they must unite their strength; and so, in the various trades, combinations of workers were formed, for the purpose of wringing from the employers better wages, shorter hours, and better conditions of labour generally. At first the law was all on the side of the employers; and a series of *Combination Laws* made all such unions of workers illegal. This did not prevent them from being formed; but it turned them into secret societies. In 1825, however, these laws were done away with; and from that time trade unionism steadily grew in strength and importance until it became one of the mightiest forces in the industrial life of Britain. Our Australian trade unions are modelled on the British unions.

A trade union is an association of persons who work in the same trade. Its principal aims are those already mentioned—to secure fair wages; moderate hours of work; healthy, safe, and pleasant conditions of work; for these things it is prepared to fight. To be able to fight, it requires money; therefore every member is required to make a regular contribution to the funds of the union. Those funds it uses, partly for the support of its members at times when they cannot get work except on terms which the union will not allow them to accept, partly for the support of members and their families in cases of sickness or accident; they are thus friendly societies. The affairs of the union are managed by a committee, or *executive*, chosen by the whole union. Most unions have branches, which manage their own affairs in detail; but the funds of the union are controlled by the central executive. The great weapon of the trade union—the weapon which it seldom uses but always holds in reserve—is the "strike,"—that is, the refusal of its members to work until the employers remove some grievance or grievances. But just as a strong nation does not often go to war, because it finds a threat of war sufficient to enforce its will, so a strong union often finds the mere threat of a strike sufficient to effect its purpose. A strike is a war; and, like every other war, it always causes loss to both sides, and generally much misery. Moreover, a strike, though it may result in a rise of wages in one trade, may cause great loss to the workers in other trades, and may lower the general level of wages. Therefore a union, if it has a wise executive, will regard the strike as a last resort, and will use it only after all other methods have failed. The strike, though it has undoubtedly played a useful part, is a barbarous method of settling a quarrel. We shall see, presently, some devices by means of which, in Australia, government has tried to make strikes unnecessary.

It must be said that the *industrial legislation* of which the last chapter told you something,—the interference of government in matters of industry,—is mainly due to the efforts of trade unions. Government did not step in to fight for the workers until some, at least, of the workers had shown that they could fight for themselves. Strong trade unions, sometimes by means of strikes, always by having in the background the power of striking, won for themselves higher wages, shorter hours, and other benefits. Then government came in and, by means of laws, extended those benefits to workers in other trades; workers who, for one reason or another, were not powerful enough, even when they united, to enforce their demands.

Victoria has the honour of having led the way in this matter of trade unionism; the first union in Australia having been formed by the stone-masons in 1850. New South Wales had a union of engineers in the following year.

The chief object of the early Australian unions was not the raising of wages, but the shortening of the hours of work. They fought for what is called the "eight hours principle,"—the limiting of the working week to forty-eight hours. It is more than fifty years since the masons, bricklayers, and others connected with the building trade, got their way in this matter; it is their victory which we celebrate on the public holiday which we call "Eight Hours' Day,"—the 21st of April. As soon as they had won this victory, unions were formed in many other trades, and the eight hours' principle was extended to them. Although there is still no law limiting the hours of work, so far as *men* are concerned, yet the principle of a working week of forty-eight hours has prevailed in the great majority of trades throughout Australia. Needless to say, however, the shortening of the hours of work was only the first thing the unions strove for; they have striven for, and won, many other benefits, including the raising of wages. Almost everything that the early unions demanded has been granted by the employers.

To bring this about, it was necessary, not merely that a union of men, in this or that trade, should be formed; but that a *union of unions* should be formed; so that each union might be backed by the strength of all the rest. In each of the Australian states there is a Trades and Labour Council,—a kind of industrial parliament, to which all the unions in the state send representatives, and which looks after the interests of unionists generally. When we look at all that trade unionism has done for the workers, we see a great example of the strength to be found in collective action, the strength that is given to an association of men working together for a common purpose; even though it be an association very much smaller than that great society which we call "the community."

Can the community, by means of its machine of government, do anything to regulate wages, and so settle industrial quarrels without strikes, which are undoubtedly a far from perfect method? For a long time it was held—and some people still hold—that the state ought not to interfere at all in the matter of wages; that such interference must always do more harm than good. Whether this view be right or wrong, we in Australia have not accepted it; we have believed that government can, and therefore ought to, do something to ensure to the labourer a fair reward for his labour. Accordingly, in all the states except Tasmania, some kind of machinery has been set up for the purpose of regulating wages. In most of the states this machinery consists of *Wages Boards*; the Commonwealth has an *Arbitration Court* for settling disputes which extend beyond the limits of one state.

The wages board system, as it works in Victoria—which was the first Australian state to introduce it—may be described in a few words. If the employers or employees in any particular trade wish government to interfere in the matter of wages, they petition parliament to give them a board. If both houses of parliament agree that it is really required, a board is appointed for that trade. It consists of not fewer than four and not more than ten members; half of the members are chosen by the employers, the other half by the employees. When the members have been chosen, they themselves choose a chairman—not from among their own number, but from outside. (The wages board is thus simply a committee, on which the two sides—employers and employees—are equally represented, with a chairman to decide between them if they cannot agree.) The board then meets and—after much discussion and hearing of evidence—fixes the lowest rate of pay to be given in each class of work in the trade. The board's decision has the force of law, and those who disobey it may be punished as if they had broken any other law. In Victoria the wages boards, though they help to make strikes unnecessary, do not make strikes illegal.

The Commonwealth court, which settles disputes extending beyond the boundaries of one state, is called the Conciliation and Arbitration Court; it consists of a judge of the High Court of Australia, who is called the President of the court. His duty is first to try conciliation,—that is, to bring about a friendly agreement between the two parties; but if conciliation fails, then he must have recourse to arbitration,—that is, he must decide between the two sides, and fix what he considers a fair rate of wages. Employers and employees may, without going to any court at all, settle all matters in dispute between them, making what is called an *industrial agreement*; they may then *register* this agreement,—which means that government gives it the force of law, so that both parties are thenceforth bound to abide by it and may be punished for breaking it. Wages boards and arbitration courts have the power of lowering wages as well as of raising them; but, as a matter of fact, they always raise wages. Mr. Justice Higgins, the President of the Commonwealth Arbitration Court, recently said of his court what is true of all this machinery for regulating wages: "Although in theory there is a power to decrease wages, in every case which has come before my predecessor or myself the Court has had to interfere by way of *increase*. The reason seems to be that the employer needs no court to enable him to reduce wages; he has simply to refuse to give employment at wages which he thinks to be too high."

CHAPTER XIX.

IMMIGRATION.

One of the most important problems with which government, in Australia, has to deal, is the problem of getting people into the country,—the problem of immigration. To understand its importance, you must realise that Australia is by far the emptiest of all the continents. It is a continent of vast unpeopled spaces. The total area of the Commonwealth is almost 3,000,000 square miles; and the total population is somewhere about 4,500,000. This works out at less than two persons per square mile; whereas in Great Britain there are 367 persons per square mile, and in Germany 297. Even these figures do not give us a true idea of how thinly-populated our country is; we have to add the fact that of our total population an astonishingly great proportion is crowded into a few large cities. Thus, more than one-third of the inhabitants of New South Wales live in Sydney; nearly half of the population of Victoria is gathered together in Melbourne, and nearly half of the population of South Australia in Adelaide. Remember, also, that the great majority of the Australian people live on a mere fringe of the continent,—along the east and south-east coasts, and in a corner of the south-west. That is the first thing, then, to bear in mind,—the *emptiness* of our country.

We must remember, too, that the vast spaces, which are at present uninhabited, are by no means uninhabitable. It used to be thought that the mere fringe I have spoken of was the only part of Australia of which much use could be made; and that the whole interior of the continent was a dry desert, fit for neither man nor beast. It is true that the farther you go from the coast, the less rainfall do you find; and without water, agriculture is impossible. But there are immense areas still unused in which the rainfall is quite sufficient for successful agriculture; and land which was once thought fit only to carry a few sheep is now being shown to be capable of yielding magnificent crops of wheat. Moreover, new methods in agriculture are enabling us, more and more, to do without a heavy rainfall; the method known as "dry farming" is one instance, and irrigation is another. It would be rash to say that *any* part of Australia is not fit to be brought under cultivation; and, at any rate, it is true that immense areas, at present unused, are perfectly fit to be used. There, then, are two facts: Australia is an almost empty continent, and it is a continent fit to maintain a vast population.

That being so, one of our pressing needs is the need of people,—people to fill our empty spaces, and to till our untilled lands, and generally to use the resources of the country. There was a time when it was common to hear men speaking as if bringing more people to Australia meant making us all poorer; as if there were just a certain amount of wealth in the country, and if more people came to share it with us, there would be so much the less for each of us. But most people now see that this is not so; that every hard-working and intelligent citizen, if his work be rightly directed, produces wealth, not for himself only but for the whole community; that the prosperity of the country depends on having sufficient population in it. Every new farmer who comes to the country helps to provide a market for the manufacturer in the city; and every new factory hand helps to provide a market for the farmer. Moreover, remember that every newcomer is an additional taxpayer; he helps to pay the expenses of government, and so makes it more possible for government to do public work which is wanted by the whole community. And there is one piece of public work, especially, which he makes it possible for government to do properly; and that is defence. To defend this great continent costs a great deal of money, and government cannot find the money without a great many taxpayers. And, as we shall see presently, a citizen does not merely pay money for the defence of his country; he can defend it directly, if he is fit to handle a rifle.

This brings us to what is perhaps the chief reason for thinking immigration a thing vitally important for the welfare of Australia. On the one hand, the older countries of the world are over-crowded; their people are crying out for room to live; and many every day are leaving their shores in search of less crowded countries, where they can have a bit of land of their own and a chance of making a decent living by tilling it. On the other hand, here is Australia,—a continent, as we have just noted, of vast unpeopled spaces, a continent with room and to spare for many additional millions of inhabitants. Would we have any right to sit down round the edge of this continent and say to those crowded countries—"Yes, we admit that this is an empty country, but we prefer to keep it so. We are very comfortable as we are, and we do not intend to let anyone else in?" If we were foolish enough to wish to do this, would we have the power? How long would the world allow us to keep our country empty? Only so long as Great Britain was willing, and able, to defend us from attack; but would Great Britain have any right to protect us if we pursued so selfish a policy?

At any rate, that is not our policy; we do not keep people out; we are anxious that people should come in. But what we do desire is to be able to choose our immigrants; we wish to make sure that the future Australian nation shall be of a certain quality; we wish to keep out people who, as we think, are of the wrong kind. And this brings us to a question of which you have often heard—the question of a "White Australia." If Australians are united in nothing else, they are united in their determination to preserve a "White Australia"[8]—to keep Australia as a heritage for white men, and not for black or brown or

---

8   The term "White Australia" reflects outdated racial attitudes from the early 1900s. These views are preserved here only for historical accuracy and do not represent contemporary Australian values.

yellow men. That is, immigration. We are determined, if we possibly can, to admit Europeans only, and to keep out Asiatics. Why?

It is high time we gave up the foolish habit of speaking about "superior" and "inferior" races, and of thinking that everyone of European descent is somehow superior to anyone of Asiatic descent. More foolish still, perhaps, is the habit of calling Asiatics "uncivilized." In her recent war with Russia, Japan showed herself, not merely a great fighter, but a highly civilized nation; in the care and skill which they devoted to their sick and wounded, the Japanese set a model for the rest of the world to copy if it can. If you had ever studied the works of some of the Indian philosophers, if you had ever read translations of the best Chinese poetry, if you had ever looked at the beautiful paintings of the great Japanese artists, you would think twice before scornfully dismissing these races as "lower" than the race to which you belong. But, whether they are lower or higher, they are different; and the difference, though not easy to describe, is all-important. Their idea of civilization is not our idea, and will not fit in with our idea. It is so utterly different, that the two races could not live happily side by side; they would never form a true community. In the United States of America, there is a population of negroes living side by side with a population of white people; the result is endless unhappiness, and bitterness, and hatred. Moreover, if Asiatics were permitted to enter Australia freely, they would come in in vast numbers; "the trickle would soon become a resistless tide;" the power would, sooner or later, pass into their hands, and we should be governed according to Asiatic ideas. And we should lose many of the things we hold most dear. For instance, the Asiatic peoples do not share our idea of the value of personal liberty.

Moreover, we believe in "racial purity." The mingling of one people with another, by intermarriage, may be an exceedingly good thing—if the two peoples are more or less closely related to one another, like the English and the Germans, for example. But the mingling of two races so utterly alien to one another as we are to the Chinese or the Japanese is a bad thing. Such a mingling always leads to the creation of a mongrel people, inferior to both the parent races.

There is a simpler reason for our desire to exclude Asiatics from Australia. The Japanese or Chinese labourer can always *undersell* the European labourer; that is, sell his labour for lower wages, because he is contented with a lower standard of living. He cheerfully does without many things which we consider necessities of life, if life is to be fit for a human being. Employers of labour, each trying to produce an article more cheaply than anyone else can, would inevitably choose the man who would do the required work for the lowest wages; and the white labourer would either lose his employment or accept lower wages and a lower standard of living. This was the first objection to Asiatic immigration; it was the reason why anti-Chinese riots took place in the days of the early gold-fields, and why, later on, several of the states passed laws excluding Chinese immigrants.

Now both China and Japan are terribly overcrowded, and there can be no doubt that both those nations cast longing eyes on the vast, fertile, empty spaces of Australia. If they could help it they would not tamely submit to be shut out from such a country; we must be prepared to keep them out, if we are to maintain our ideal of a "White Australia." That they may be kept out, two things are necessary: first, the country must be properly defended—a point with which the next chapter will deal; and, secondly, those tempting empty spaces must not remain empty. We must induce white men to come to Australia. During the last ten years, Canada has induced a million and a half of people to leave their homes and settle in that country. There is no reason, except the greater distance from Europe, why Australia should not attract immigrants in the same way; Australia has a better climate than Canada has, and can offer at least as good a chance to the newcomer of earning a comfortable livelihood, and of becoming prosperous.

Immigration is dealt with both by the Commonwealth government and by the governments of the various states. To try to keep undesirable immigrants out of one state, if another allowed them to enter freely, would, as has been said already, be like putting a rabbit-proof fence half-way round your paddock; they have to be excluded from Australia as a whole, and that can be done only by one central authority. But when it comes to bringing immigrants to the country, it is another matter. It is no use bringing farmers to the country unless we have land for them to settle on; and only the states can give them land, for the land belongs to the states, not to the Commonwealth. (The states, at present, are competing with one another in the attempt to attract immigrants; Victoria, especially, has during the last few years succeeded in bringing in a great number of farmers, though not nearly so many as are needed.) What it amounts to is this: the task of the Commonwealth is to keep out the immigrants whom we do not want, while the task of the states is to bring in the immigrants whom we do want.

Asiatics are by no means the only immigrants whom we do not want. We do not want criminals, any more than we want persons suffering from infectious diseases; and it is the business of government to keep out both these classes of undesirables. We do not want persons who, for any reason, are unfit to earn their own living; such persons would only become a burden on the community, and would tend to create, in our cities, the curse of the miserable slum population so well known in the cities of the old world. Moreover, we do not want to allow employers to bring down wages by introducing cheap labour—hosts of men and women who have been taught by poverty to work for a starvation wage. Therefore, before any employer is allowed to bring into the country men or women to work on his land or in his factory, he must undertake to pay them the wages which are accepted as fair in his district. This is required by a law which the Commonwealth government has to enforce.

CHAPTER XX.

DEFENCE.

When we compare a civilised nation with a primitive or savage people, what strikes us as the main difference between them? Surely this: that among savages, brute force still prevails; among civilized people, law has, to a great extent, taken the place of brute force. When two savages quarrel, they settle the matter by fighting; when two citizens of a civilized nation quarrel, there is a law to which they can appeal, and a judge who will decide between them. That is one of the meanings of "civilization,"—doing away with violence, and the setting up of reason and justice in its place. But when we turn from the relations between one citizen and another to the relation between one nation and another, we find a strange and surprising contrast. We find that we have gone back, at one stride, from civilization to savagery; we find even the most highly civilized nations behaving towards one another like primitive savages. If two nations quarrel, there is no judge to whom they can appeal; there is no law to prevent them from flying at one another's throats; there is nothing but brute force to decide between them. Civilization has taught us to prevent the stronger citizen from trampling on the weaker citizen; it has not yet shown us how to prevent the stronger nation from trampling on the weaker nation. A citizen feels quite safe in the streets of his city; he does not think it necessary to arm himself even with a walking-stick; but a nation does not feel safe unless it is armed to the teeth. In Europe, at the present day, we see the sorry spectacle of great nations straining every nerve to become fit for the ancient and barbarous test of a nation's strength,—the test of battle; spending vast sums of money every year on their armies and navies; constantly inventing and making new instruments of destruction,— new battle-ships to carry death more swiftly, new explosives to carry it farther, new submarines to hurl it upwards from the depths of the sea, new air-ships to drop it down out of the skies. This seems, and is, a barbarous state of things, and we may all join in fervently hoping that some day it may be put an end to; but meanwhile we must face the fact that the world rings with preparations for war, and that the great nations keep an unwinking watch on one another, and hold themselves in constant readiness for action; like the knights in Scott's poem,—

> *They lie down to rest with corslet laced,*
> *Pillowed on buckler cold and hard;*
> *They carve at the meal with gloves of steel,*
> *And drink the red wine thro' the helmet barr'd.*

Britain long ago perceived that a navy was what she chiefly needed for her protection. The continental nations of Europe had to expect attacks by land; they had to guard their land frontiers, and for that purpose they required immense armies. But Britain was an island state, and could be attacked only by sea; therefore a navy, rather than an army, was what she required. To this day the British army is insignificant compared with the mighty hosts of France or Germany; but the British navy is by far the greatest in the world. For, now that Britain is no longer an island state, but a world-wide Empire, her need of a strong navy is greater than ever; it is vital to her very existence. It is felt that Britain is not safe unless she has a navy stronger than any two other navies combined; for she must be ready to defend herself not merely against any hostile power, but against any probable combination of hostile powers. (It is possible,

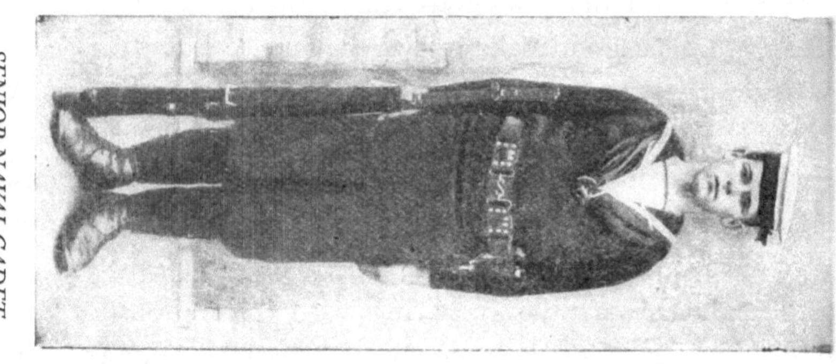

SENIOR NAVAL CADET.

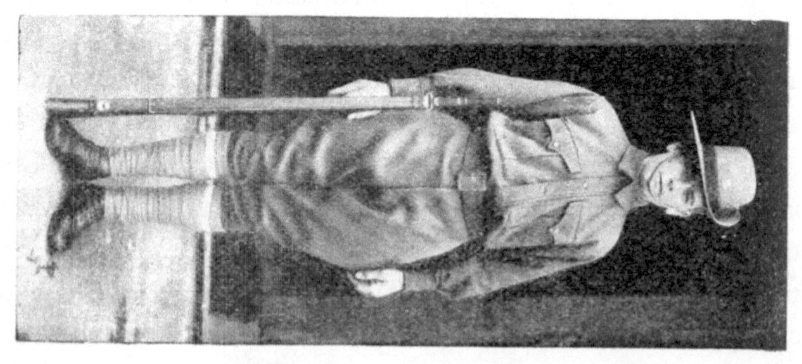

SENIOR MILITARY CADET.

of course, that more than two nations might combine against her, but it is not probable.) It is necessary to Britain's very existence as a great nation that she should have, and hold, the *command of the sea;* that is to say, that she should be able to protect her *trade routes* in every ocean.

To understand why this is necessary, you must remember that Britain is a very small country with a very large population, and that of this population a great proportion is engaged in manufactures. Now Britain cannot produce her own "raw material," as we call the stuff, whatever it may be, out of which manufactured articles are made; more than two-thirds of her raw material is brought to her across the seas. (In Lancashire, for example, hundreds of thousands of persons are employed in the manufacture of cotton cloth: the raw cotton cannot be grown in England, but must be brought from overseas.) Nor can Britain produce anything like a proper supply of food for her immense population; a large part of her food-supply also comes to her from overseas. Every day of the year, along those great ocean highways which we call the trade routes, thousands of ships are steaming or sailing to and fro; some carrying to Britain her food and her raw material, some carrying from Britain to distant parts of the world the products of her industry. Now try to imagine what would happen if, even for a few days, England were unable to protect her trade routes; if, even for a few days, an enemy's fleet were able to cut off her supplies of raw material and of food. The manufacturing industries would be brought to a standstill; millions would be thrown out of employment; they would have no money to buy food, even if food remained cheap; but, at the same time, the price of food would rise to such heights that only the rich could buy. The great mass of the population would be plunged into literal starvation; to prevent which calamity, Britain would have to surrender at once, and accept whatever terms the enemy chose to offer. An uninterrupted supply of raw materials and of foodstuffs is as necessary to Britain's existence as an uninterrupted supply of air is necessary to your existence and to mine. No other nation in the world is in the same position. The very life of Britain depends on her being the unassailable mistress of the seas.

But, during recent years, various foreign nations have been making tremendous efforts to build up for themselves great navies; and to maintain her supremacy Britain has been forced to make efforts more tremendous still. In one single year she now spends—on her navy alone, and putting her army on one side—the gigantic sum of more than £40,000,000. You will realise with what costly weapons a modern nation fights, when you are told that a single British battleship, like the famous *Dreadnought*, costs a great fortune—almost £2,000,000—to build; yet even such a battleship lasts only for a few years, after which time it becomes old-fashioned and has to be set aside as practically useless. Britain has to be constantly building new battleships, as well as cruisers, destroyers, torpedo-boats, submarines, and all the other parts of a modern navy.

Why does Britain spend these vast sums every year on her navy? Is it because she loves fighting?—or because she loves display and cutting a great figure in the world?—or because she is greedy of power and wishes to trample on the other nations? For none of these reasons. We must look upon the money she spends on defence as being paid for *insurance*. The merchant pays a certain sum every year to a Fire Insurance Company, which undertakes, in return for those payments, to make good his loss if his warehouse should be burnt down; he insures his goods, to save himself from the risk of ruin; and it is to save herself from the risk of ruin that Britain bears the heavy and ever-increasing burden of a navy strong enough to ward off any probable blow.

Now you may possibly ask what all this has to do with Australia; but I have already reminded you of the absolute *one-ness* of the Empire, and in that fact lies the answer to your question. In the first place, the greatest part of Australia's *trade* is with the United Kingdom; and therefore the commercial ruin of Britain would mean widespread ruin in Australia. But that, important as it is, is not the most important point. The most important point—looking at the matter selfishly—is that the ruin of Britain would mean the ruin of the power which defends Australia from foreign attack.

Until quite lately, Britain bore practically the whole burden of defending the Empire; and she still bears, and will for many a year continue to bear, by far the greatest part of that burden. If she were decisively defeated at sea, and had to make peace with her enemy on that enemy's own terms, one of those terms would almost certainly be, that she must give up some part of the Empire,—perhaps Australia; and so our country would pass into foreign hands. But even if this were not made one of the conditions of peace, still, if the British fleet were defeated, every part of the Empire would lie open to the attack of the victorious enemy; he could embark a large army and take possession of the Dominions one by one. If we value our freedom, then the supremacy of Britain at sea is a matter of as much interest to us as to Britain herself. Until quite lately, as I have said, the Dominions left the British taxpayer to bear almost the whole burden of defence. In 1908, for instance, Britain spent more than £32,000,000 on naval defence alone; Australia spent only a little more than £250,000; and Canada spent nothing at all. But the feeling has grown up, that each of the self-governing dominions ought to carry its fair share of the burden, since the benefits of defence are shared by all. Even so late as 1910, however, Australia was paying, for naval and military defence, only about 7/- per inhabitant, while Britain was paying about £1 8s. per inhabitant. But Australia has now made a start with a navy of her own, and she has also provided for the formation of a citizen army. She began her navy with the purchase of three destroyers.

If you ever get a chance of looking over one of these ships, the

THE BEGINNINGS OF OUR NAVY.

beginnings of the Australian navy, you should take it; and you should remember what they stand for. They do not stand for Australia's power to defend herself; they stand for Australia's power, and resolve, to *help* in the defence of the Empire. Foolish people sometimes speak as if, in the event of war, it would be the duty of those ships of ours to hang about our coasts and defend Australia. Their duty would be, to be a part of the British navy, and to play their part in the work of that navy in whatever part of the world they were required. It is that navy, as a whole, that we depend on; if it were decisively beaten, though it were ten thousand miles away, the presence of our destroyers would not help us. You cannot be reminded too often of the fact that Australia is strong only in the strength of the British Empire; cut off from the Empire, she would be as powerless as a hand cut off from the body. She could, of her own unaided strength, no more defend herself against one of the powerful nations than a mouse could defend itself against a lion. A high authority has told us that Australia's proper share of the burden of Naval defence would be £4,000,000 per year; but some people doubt whether the country could bear that strain. Well, even if she can afford so much, what chance do you think she would have, in the long run, against a power like Germany, which can afford to spend in one year more than £20,000,000 on her navy and more than £40,000,000 on her army?

Australia's navy, then, represents her determination to pay her share of the cost of defending the Empire. Her army represents her belief, that it is every citizen's duty to bear arms in defence of his country if it should be invaded. All male citizens of the Commonwealth, between the ages of eighteen and sixty, may be called upon by government to serve as soldiers in time of war. But a person who has not been trained may be worse than useless as a soldier; therefore the Commonwealth government—which has charge of defence—insists that the proper training shall be given to all. Boys who have reached the age of twelve must begin to drill; from the age of fourteen to eighteen, they are given more advanced military drill, and are taught to shoot; from eighteen to twenty-five, they must spend a fixed number of days in camp, completing their training. The government has established a military college, for the training of officers to command the citizen army; and it has also made provision for the manufacture of guns and ammunition. If Britain were at war, even though she were not defeated, she might be for a time unable to defend Australia against a raid by a foreign foe. In such an event, it would be the duty of Australian citizens, acting together as a trained army, to defend their country.

Here, again, we see that the work of government means compulsion. We are *obliged* to undergo military training, and we are *obliged* to pay taxes for the keeping up of the navy. Is this an interference with freedom? Or is it, rather, a recognition that freedom is a precious thing, and that it is the duty of every citizen of a free country to be ready to take up arms in defence of his country's freedom?

CHAPTER XXI

TAXATION

If you have read the preceding chapters with attention, you have begun to have some idea of the enormous amount and variety of work carried on by a modern government; and this implies an enormous expenditure of money. The tools of government,—the great public buildings, the post-offices and prisons, the battle-ships and the forts, the railway lines and the roads, the telegraph-wires and the irrigation channels—all have to be bought and paid for; and vast sums have to be paid in wages to the army of men who use these tools. Did it ever occur to you to ask, where government gets the money for all this? The hero of the fairy-tale utters a magic word, and lo, a great heap of coins lies before him; or a kind fairy tells him a secret way of turning stones into gold. The story of government is in some ways more wonderful than any fairy-tale; but a government has no such magical and mysterious method of providing for its needs. Its method is very plain and simple; it demands the money it requires, and gets it, from the people for whom it does the work. We all contribute to the cost of governing the country.

(The money a government receives each year, to enable it to carry on its work, is called its annual *revenue*. A few figures may help you to an idea of what government costs. The revenue of the Commonwealth government for a single year (the year ending June 30th, 1909) was £14,350,793. The six State governments, for the same year, had a total revenue of £34,457,640. And the revenue of the municipal governments throughout the six states, for the year 1908, was £5,391,585.)

Our chief contributions to the cost of government are called *taxes*; or, in the case of the municipalities, they are called *rates*; there is no real difference between rates and taxes. It is true that these are not our only contributions; for instance, every time we pay for a railway ticket, we are contributing to the cost of government; but that is not usually called a tax; it is simply a definite price paid for a definite service—being carried in the train for a certain distance,— just as we pay the grocer a definite sum for a pound of sugar. The difference may be made clearer by a reference to two kinds of penny stamps,—duty-stamps, for putting on receipts, and postage-stamps, for putting on letters. The price of the duty-stamp is usually called a tax; the price of the postage-stamp is not. Why? Because in return for the penny we have paid for the postage-stamp, the government performs a certain definite service for us: it carries our letter to its destination; whereas it performs no such service in return for the penny we have paid for the duty-stamp; *that* penny is just a part of what we pay for the general work of government. A tax, then, is a sum paid to a government, not as the price of any one definite service, but in return for the innumerable services which that government performs for us.

We have already seen that a modern government does many kinds of public work which ancient governments did not dream of doing; but we may be very sure that, in the most ancient times, whatever the government did or did not do, it always taxed the people. True, taxes did not always take the form of money; they often took the form of forced labour. (Even in our own time, they are not always paid in money; compulsory military service, for instance, is a form of taxation, though it is a tax on our time instead of on our money.) But the main difference lies in this fact: that ancient governments, which did little for the benefit of the people, taxed them heavily, while good modern governments, which do infinitely more for us, tax us lightly. Whenever history gives us a glimpse of the life of an ancient nation, we find the mass of the people groaning under an intolerable burden of taxation. And indeed we need not go very far back in history to find an example of such a state of things; France, for instance, was in that condition until, at the end of the eighteenth century, the people rose in revolt and took terrible vengeance on their oppressors. It is now universally recognised that a good government taxes as lightly as possible; and we, in Australia, have no reason to complain of the cost of government. We pay surprisingly little, considering all we get in return. Of course you occasionally hear a man grumbling at the amount he has to pay in rates and taxes; but let such a man sit down and carefully add up all that he has to pay, and then, with equal care, add up all the benefits he receives. Let him steadily reflect on what his life would be like if there were no government,—no roads, no public schools, no police, no law-courts, no post-office, no care for public health, and so on; and let him ask himself whether he would not cheerfully pay his taxes five times over rather than be deprived of those blessings which are implied in the term "good government." We are so accustomed to those blessings that we take them for granted and grumble at having to pay for them; forgetting that our ancestors, who fought for us against tyranny and injustice centuries ago, were willing to give all they possessed—even life itself, in many cases—as the price of good government.

> *All we have of freedom, all we use or know—*
> *This our fathers bought for us long and long ago.*

Who ought to pay the taxes? At first sight this seems a very simple question: the work done by government is done for the benefit of all; therefore the taxes should be paid by all. And this is true; no-one should be allowed to escape from paying his proper share; it is when we try to find out what a man's "proper share" is, that the difficulty begins. It is a difficulty which has baffled the wisest statesmen; for no method of taxation has yet been discovered which does not involve some injustice. In a book so small as this, there is no room for a discussion of the principles of taxation; we may say, briefly, that what governments ought to aim at, and what justice demands, is *equality of burden*,—that everyone should bear an equal share of the burden. But what does this mean? Plainly, it does not mean that everyone should pay an equal sum of money, for this would not be equality of burden at all. Suppose, for instance, that every grown-up person had to pay £10 a year in taxes; to a poor man, with a large family to support, this might be an intolerably heavy burden, while to a rich man it would be no burden at all,—he would scarcely notice it. There would be no justice here, no real equality of burden. For equality of burden means equality of sacrifice, and in this case one man would have to make great sacrifices while the other man would not have to sacrifice anything.

In order to secure equality of burden, the tax would have to be in proportion to a man's ability to pay. And that is what, in Australia, we aim at. Speaking roughly, we may say that our taxes are not laid on persons, but on the wealth of the country; if you own a great deal of that wealth you are taxed heavily, if you own very little you are taxed lightly. Thus, for instance, in the case of the *municipal rates,* what you have to pay depends on the value of the house you live in or the land you own within the municipality. And so it is with the three principal taxes imposed by the different state governments. The *probate and succession duties* are taxes levied on the money or other property which a person leaves by will to his or her heirs. The land tax is a tax levied on what is called the "unimproved value" of a person's land; that is, its present value apart from the improvements—buildings, fences, etc.—which the owner may have put on it. The *income* tax is a tax levied on a person's yearly income. All these taxes are known as direct, and are levied by the state governments;

the Commonwealth government draws a great part of its revenue from *indirect taxation*, of which you will read presently.

But a moment's thought will show you that we have not got over our difficulty,—the difficulty of insuring that everyone shall bear an equal burden of taxation,—when we have commanded everyone to pay according to his wealth. Take, for instance, the income tax; suppose we say that everyone shall pay a shilling every year for every pound of his income. Then a man with an income of £100 a year would have to pay £5, while a man with £1,000 a year would pay £50. But it is quite plain that to a man who is struggling to keep his wife and family on £100 a year, £5 would be a very heavy burden indeed, whereas £50 would scarcely be a burden at all to a man with £1,000 a year. In two ways we try to meet this difficulty, though we cannot be said to have overcome it. In the first place, no income tax is laid on those whose income falls below a certain amount; they are declared *exempt* from this tax. In the second place, we make the tax *progressive*; that is, the proportion of tax to total income grows greater as the income increases; for example, a man may have to pay sixpence in the pound if his income is less than £500, sevenpence in the pound if his income is over £500 but less than £1,000, and so on. (The actual rates are not the same in any two states.) Even this, however, by no means secures equality of burden; as I have already told you, every tax involves some unfairness. For instance: of two men, each having an income of £500 a year, one has only himself to keep while the other supports a wife and a large family; though they pay the same tax, it cannot be said that they bear the same burden. The ideal system of taxation has not yet been discovered.

When I tell you that those whose income falls below a certain figure are exempt from taxation, you may be inclined to ask why the poor, who share in the benefits of good government, should not pay their share of the cost of government? Indeed, it may be said that it is the poor who especially gain by the protection and the help of government; we have seen that an important part of the work of government is to help the poor. And in that fact lies the answer to your question. It would plainly be very absurd if government took away with one hand what it gives with the other; if it spent money on relieving the destitute, and at the same time swelled the ranks of the destitute by taxing the poor, those who are just able to keep themselves above destitution. The poor, then, ought not to be taxed; but it is more difficult to say exactly how much property a person must have before the government should levy a tax on it. As a general principle perhaps we may say, that *taxes should be levied only on that portion of a person's property which is over and above what is required to provide himself, and those dependent on him, with the necessaries of life.* But it is not easy to say what are the necessaries of life; and our state governments get round the difficulty roughly by imposing no direct tax on incomes of less than £200 a year. (In Tasmania, £100 a year.) But even these incomes do not escape from indirect taxation.

The indirect taxes—which are the Commonwealth government's main source of revenue—are *Customs duties and Excise duties.* The customs duties are taxes which have to be paid on many different kinds of goods imported into this country from other countries. Some kinds of goods may be imported into Australia without the payment of any tax: these are said to be *on the free list.* Which articles shall be on the free list, which articles shall be *dutiable,* what shall be the amount of duty payable on each class of goods,—all this is settled by the Commonwealth parliament, which draws up, from time to time, a *tariff:* that is, a list of dutiable articles with the amount of duty to be paid on each. When a vessel comes into an Australian port, the cargo is examined by an officer of the customs *department* of the Commonwealth government: and the importer of dutiable articles is not allowed to remove those articles from the wharf until he has paid the duty. This is the *protective tariff policy* of Australia. Before federation came, when each of the states had to determine

A BUSY DAY IN THE CUSTOMS HOUSE.

its own tariff policy, there were many battles in the state parliaments between *protectionists* and *free-traders*, the former believing that goods imported into the country ought to be taxed, the latter holding that they ought to come in free of taxation. In those days, one Australian state could tax goods imported from another Australian state. When the Commonwealth was established, this was done away with, and *interstate free-trade* became the law; that is, all goods may pass, free of duty, from one Australian state to another. But as regards goods imported from any country outside Australia, the Commonwealth has been, from the first, a protectionist country. By the federal Constitution, the power to collect customs duties was taken away from the separate states and handed over to the Commonwealth government. The state governments have nothing to do with this form of taxation.

Customs duties provide the Commonwealth with the greatest part of its revenue; but it also draws a very considerable amount from *excise duties*; that is, from a tax levied on certain articles which are not imported into the country, but manufactured here. The articles taxed in this way are—beer, spirits, starch, sugar, and tobacco.

Why are these called *indirect* taxes? Because the persons who really pay them do not pay them *direct* to the government; they are paid in a roundabout, or indirect way. Thus: a merchant imports a large number of boots from England; he has to pay to the government a certain sum of money, a certain percentage of the value of the boots. But the importer is not the person who really pays the tax, because, in consequence of the tax, he adds a little to the price of each pair of boots; he makes the purchasers of the boots pay the tax. Thus when you buy a pair of English boots, you pay (besides the price of the boots) the tax; you pay it to the shopkeeper, and the shopkeeper pays it to the merchant who imported the boots, and the merchant pays it to the government. It passes from you to the government in an indirect way.

I have told you that it is recognised that the very poor ought not to be taxed; but as a matter of fact, no-one can altogether escape taxation,—I shall show you why. Suppose a man's income is not big enough for him to have to pay any income-tax, and suppose he owns neither house nor land, and therefore has to pay neither municipal rates nor land-tax: then he escapes direct taxation, but he does not escape indirect taxation. Every time he smokes a pipe, he is paying an indirect tax, because his tobacco would not have cost him so much if it had not been for the duty on tobacco. And even if he manages—which is very improbable—to do without using any article on which duty has to be paid, he still pays taxes. For instance, he pays a certain rent for the house he lives in; rents would be lower if the owners of houses had no taxes to pay; so that in paying his rent he is helping the owner to pay taxes. The whole cost of living would be lower, for him, if the people from whom he buys things had no taxes to pay. Taxes, by the difference they make in prices, spread themselves over the whole community.

It is worth noticing, that a tax, besides bringing in revenue, may have many other results; and a government may impose a tax, not because it is in need of revenue, but for some quite different reason. Thus, for example, a government may impose a land tax, not because it needs the money, but because it thinks a tax will force the owners of large stretches of land to break up their estates into small blocks and sell or let them to farmers. Again, a government may impose heavy customs duties, and heavy excise duties, on wine, beer, and spirits, not for the purpose of increasing its revenue but for the purpose of lessening drunkenness. Again—and this is the most important example—a government may impose heavy customs duties on a certain manufactured article, not because it wants the money, but because it wants to encourage the manufacture of that article within the country. This is the meaning of the term *protective tariff*; it is intended, not merely to bring in revenue, but to *protect* the local manufacturer. Some people in Australia think the tariff ought to be as low as possible,—just high enough to bring in sufficient revenue to the government; others think it ought to be much higher than this,—high enough to protect the Australian manufacturer against the competition of manufacturers in other countries. But this is a question far too complicated for us to discuss here.

There is one other thing to remember about taxation, and it is this: that the power to tax is one of the powers of the legislature; no-one can demand from you a single penny, by way of tax, unless the legislature has first made it law. If you have read your history of Britain you will remember that this was one of the principal reasons why the English fought for representative government, and that it was only after a very long and stubborn contest that they established their right to be taxed only by men whom they themselves chose as their representatives. And I need not remind you that this question of taxation was the main cause of the quarrel which resulted in Britain's loss of her American colonies. It is now regarded as a fundamental principle of the British constitution, and of all constitutions modelled on the British, that *only Parliament has a right to tax the People.*

PART III.
ORGANS OF GOVERNMENT.

Having looked at some of the principal kinds of public work done by governing bodies in Australia, let us now inquire what sort of things these "governing bodies" are, and how they do their work. In other words, we have now to try to understand the *structure of government*. In another little book (*The Struggle for Freedom*) I have described the birth and gradual growth of Parliament, and given some account of the Party System, and of the Cabinet. I shall assume that you know (from that book or from some other) the outlines of the story of how Parliament became what it is; and in the following pages I shall confine myself to a brief description of the machinery of government as it exists in Australia at the present time.

CHAPTER XXII.

THE LEGISLATURE.

Just as the human body does its work by means of various *organs*,—the seeing eye, the thinking brain, the stomach which digests food, the heart which sends the blood flowing through arteries and veins, and so forth,—so we may speak of the organs, three in number, by which government does its work: the *legislature*, or law-making organ; the *judiciary*, the organ which applies the law to particular cases; and the *executive*, the organ which enforces the law, and which carries on public work in general. Let us take the legislature first. In a self-governing country, the legislature is *Parliament*.

The parliaments of the Commonwealth and of all the Australian states are modelled very closely on the parliament of Britain. In Britain, Parliament consists of the King, the House of Lords, and the House of Commons. So an Australian parliament (federal or state) consists of the King's representative (Governor-General or Governor), an Upper House, and a Lower House.

We shall return later to the question, what part is played by the King or the King's representative in the business of governing; meanwhile, let me remind you of two great contests in the history of Parliament. First, there was the great and grim struggle for supremacy between Parliament and the King; a struggle which seemed, under the despotic Tudor sovereigns, to have ended in a victory for the monarchy; which began again under the Stuarts, grew even more bitter and violent, and became a struggle to the death; and which may be said to have ended, in a complete victory for Parliament, with the Revolution of 1688. After that date a second long contest took place to decide the question whether the House of Commons was to be really representative of the whole people, or only of a small group of rich and powerful persons; this contest practically came to an end with the Reform Act of 1832, though later acts of the same nature were required to make the people's victory complete. Lately there has been, in Britain, a third struggle, to decide whether the will of the House of Commons should be supreme or whether it could be withstood by the House of Lords; perhaps it is too soon to say that this struggle is yet ended, but an act passed in 1911 seems to secure that, if the Lower House is resolutely bent on a certain course of action, its will shall prevail.

The result of the *second* struggle is, that the House of Commons now rests "on a democratic basis";—that is to say, the great mass of the nation elects the members of that House. The same thing may be said of *both* houses of the Commonwealth parliament, and of the *lower* house in each of the six states. Practically every grown-up person living in Australia has a voice in choosing the members of the Commonwealth parliament, and in choosing the members of the lower house of the parliament of his or her state. Remember, then, that when you are grown up, if you are not so unfortunate as to be the inmate of a lunatic asylum, or of a gaol, it will be your right and your duty, again and again, to give your voice in the choosing of a Member of Parliament; in other words, to *vote at an* election.

As to the Upper House, you know, of course, that in Great Britain it is not *elected* at all; it is an *hereditary* house,—the majority of its members are members because their fathers were members before them; the remainder are there because they have been made Peers of the realm (or Bishops of the church) by a Prime Minister; nobody sits in that house because he was chosen by the people. In the Commonwealth parliament, the members of the upper house are chosen by the same people who choose the members of the lower house; i.e., by the grown-up citizens (men and women) of Australia. In four out of the six states, the upper house is also chosen by the citizens; not, however, by *all* the citizens, but only by such as possess property of a certain value. (The amount varies in the different states.) In the other two states, New South Wales and Queensland, the upper house is not "elective" but "nominated"; that is to say, its members are not chosen by the people at all, but are appointed (for life) by the State Governor, acting on the advice of the Ministry. With these two exceptions, all the Australian houses of parliament are *elective*,—they are chosen by the people. The choosing of the members of a house of parliament is called an *election*.

A parliamentary election is a very simple matter. Suppose, for instance, it is the lower house of a State parliament that has to be elected. The state has been divided into *electorates*, each electorate having the right to choose one man to represent it in parliament. For some time before the election day, the rival *candidates*—the men who wish to be chosen by your electorate,—go about the district explaining at public meetings their political views; so that you have many chances of comparing the candidates and deciding which of them you ought to vote for. When the election day arrives, you go to the nearest of the *polling-booths*, the places set apart, here and there in the electorate, for the recording of votes,—and there you are given a small piece of paper, with the names of the candidates printed on it; you put a mark opposite the name of the man whom you wish to see elected[9], drop the paper into a box, and—that is all; you have recorded your vote. How simple it all seems, how trivial and insignificant! Yet you have exercised one of the most important privileges of citizenship. The right to put that mark on that slip of paper would never have been yours if, at various periods of Britain's

9   See Appendix: Preferential Voting.

history, thousands of obscure and forgotten men had not been willing to throw away ease and comfort and even life itself in the struggle with tyranny. We are very unworthy of our forefathers if we take this privilege lightly; for they did not win it lightly. A right always implies a duty, you will find; and the right to vote implies the duty of voting carefully and thoughtfully and after due consideration.

But how are you really to decide which candidate you ought to vote for? Well, as we have just noted, you can go and hear the candidates speak, and after carefully listening to them both (if there are two) you may come to the conclusion that A is a better man, or an abler man, than B, and you may therefore decide to vote for A. But in a modern election, the voter as a rule asks himself, not "which *man* would I rather see in parliament?" but "which *party* would I rather see in power?" And the candidate, in his public speeches, does not merely explain his own personal views; he explains the views of the party to which he belongs. It is between parties rather than between men that you have to judge.

You already understand what the *party system* means; but I may just briefly remind you that, in all parliaments modelled on the British, the proper working of the machine depends on the members dividing themselves into at least two groups or parties. There may be more than two; in the British House of Commons at the present moment there are four parties, if not five; but there must be at least two. There are two clearly-defined parties at present in each of the Australian parliaments. Now each of the candidates who comes to your electorate will tell you clearly of which party he will be a member if he is elected. Your business is, then, to find out what are the views of each party, and what are their differences. When you have found this out, you will probably find that you agree with one party on some points, with the other party on some other points; and you will have to decide which party you agree with *on what you consider the most important points*. For instance, if you were in England just now, you might possibly think the Unionist party right in opposing Home Rule for Ireland, and the Liberal party right in opposing a protective tariff for Great Britain; if so, whether you voted for a Liberal or a Unionist candidate would depend on whether you thought the Irish question or the Tariff question the more important. In other words, you have to ask yourself which party, on the whole, you wish to see governing your country. For the country is governed, as we shall see presently, by the leaders of that party which has the greater number of members in the lower house of parliament. If you think A's party would govern the state much better than B's party, you will vote for A, even though you may think B an abler man than A.

There are various ways of finding out what the views of the different parties are. One way is to read the newspapers carefully. But the best way of all is to attend the meetings at which the candidates speak, and to listen attentively to what *both* candidates have to say; for you ought to hear both sides of a question before making up your mind. In Australia at the present time there are persons who condemn a candidate without hearing him; and not only do they refuse to listen to him, but they try to prevent him from being heard by anyone. They come to his meetings for the purpose of drowning his voice by shouting and stamping. Such men are bad citizens; they could give no clearer proof that they are unworthy of the right of voting.

So far we have been speaking about an election to the *lower house.* The upper house remains to be considered; and at this point it may occur to you to ask, why we require an upper house at all. Why should not parliament consist of one house only? The answer to this question will be more easily understood if you first understand clearly *how parliament makes the laws.*

When it is proposed to make a new law or to alter an old one, the proposal is called a *bill*; and the member of parliament who makes the proposal is said to *introduce a bill*. A bill may be introduced in either of the two houses, except bills relating to taxation or the spending of money: these must be introduced in the lower house. (This rule is of course of great importance in Great Britain, for it means that control of the people's money belongs to the house elected by the people. In the Commonwealth parliament, when *both* houses are elected by the people, it is not of such vital importance.) The member who wishes to make the proposal first asks the house for permission to introduce the bill, and when this is granted, he moves *that the bill be read a first time*. As a rule this is granted without debate; and then an officer of parliament—the Clerk—reads the title of the bill aloud. (Long ago, the Clerk used to read the whole bill aloud, but nowadays this would be a great waste of time, since the bill is printed and members can read it for themselves.) Some time is then allowed for members to study the bill; then the member in charge of it moves *that it be read a second time*. Before this is granted, a debate very often takes place; a discussion, not of small details in the bill, but of its general principles. If a majority of members approve of its general principles, the motion is carried, and the bill is supposed to have been read a second time. Then follows a discussion of the bill in all its details, for which purpose the house is said to resolve itself into a committee; this only means that the discussion is more informal, more like an ordinary conversation, than a regular debate is. When this discussion is over, and the bill has been gone through clause by clause, and all suggested alterations have been either agreed to or set aside, the *third reading* is proposed. At this stage the house considers the bill again as a whole, and decides whether it ought or ought not to become a law. If passed through the third reading, the bill is sent to the other house, where the whole process is repeated from beginning to end. If the other house decides to accept the bill, but with certain amendments, the bill thus amended is sent back to the first house, which has to decide whether it can accept these amendments. If the bill passes successfully through both houses, it has then to receive the Royal assent. In Australia, of course, that means that it has to receive the assent of the Governor-General (in the case of the Commonwealth parliament), or of a state Governor (in the case of one of the state parliaments). When it has received the Royal assent, it is no longer a bill: it is now an Act of Parliament, and is placed on the statute-book as one of the laws of the land.

CHAPTER XXIII.

THE LEGISLATURE (continued).

We may now return to the question suggested in the last chapter,—
What is the use of an upper house?

And first, notice one striking fact. We can quite easily understand
why the Imperial Parliament has its upper house, the House of Lords.
The British constitution was not made; it grew; it has been growing
for centuries; and it contains many things which are of great antiquity.
Among these is the House of Lords; it is directly descended from
the Great Council of powerful barons which surrounded the Norman Kings of England; and this, in turn, was descended from the
Witenagemot, the assembly of "wise men," on whose advice and help
the Anglo-Saxon monarchs leaned. It would have taken a revolution
to get rid of this ancient institution. Many Englishmen have desired
it to be abolished, as a thing which had outlived its usefulness and
had become simply a nuisance. But the striking fact is that in new
countries, where a wholly new constitution had to be devised, and
where there was no ancient aristocracy to form an upper house,
the men who devised the new constitutions devised an imitation
of the House of Lords. Thus, for instance, in the United States of
America, there is an upper house, both in the Federal parliament and
in the parliament of each state. And so it is in all the self-governing
dominions of the Empire: each of them has its imitation House of
Lords, its upper house. Why is this?

Well, the most obvious use of an upper house is that it tends to prevent laws from being made in a hurry. We have just seen that, before a proposal becomes law, it has to be agreed to, in identical terms, by both houses; and this means, if it means nothing else, that a law cannot be made without more time and thought and discussion being given to it than would be given by a parliament consisting of one house alone. George Washington gave a capital illustration of the use of an upper house. When the American constitution was being devised, a young man asked Washington, at a tea-table, why parliament should have two houses. Pointing to the saucer into which the young man had emptied his tea-cup, "That," said Washington, "is the use of an upper house. It is something into which we pour our legislation to cool." When we drink our tea too hot, we are apt to regret it, when it is too late. It very often happens that a person is carried away by passion into doing things which he regrets when it is too late; and a nation is very like a person in this respect; a whole nation is sometimes carried away by passion. "Experience," it has been said, "seems to have led modern democracies to fear a too great facility for translating the impulse of the moment into law." That is why the legislatures in almost all democratic countries nowadays consist of two houses.

The members of the House of Lords are not, like the members of the lower house, dependent on public approval for their seats in parliament; public disapproval cannot unseat them; they are therefore the more ready to face unpopularity and to set their faces against the people's will if they think it right to do so. In the long run, the people's will must always prevail, but the House of Lords can exercise a restraining influence, and prevent a law from being made in a hurry. The House of Lords has always been slow, cautious, opposed to rash changes.

Now in the Australian states the upper houses, though they do not consist of hereditary peers, are still a little more likely to oppose the popular impulses than the lower houses are. In two of the states, as we have seen, they are not dependent on public approval, for they are not elected by the people. In the other four states, they are elected, but not by the whole people; only by those who possess some property. Moreover, to be a member of the upper house, you must possess property. And people who possess property are proverbially more inclined to prudence and caution than those who have nothing. Moreover, the members of an upper house do not all retire at the same time; they retire in turn, so that the house as a whole is never dissolved; and this also tends to make it more independent of the people's whims.

In the Commonwealth parliament, the upper house is more democratic than in the state parliament, for it is elected by the voters who elect the lower house,—that is, by the mass of the people. And the upper house in this instance has not turned out to be more prudent and cautious than the lower house. But, even here, the fact that there are two houses is a guarantee that legislation will not be so hasty and impulsive as if there were only one.

In the states, the upper house is called the Legislative Council and the lower the Legislative Assembly. In the Commonwealth, the upper house is called the Senate and the lower the House of Representatives. There is no very good reason for calling one house the "Senate"; both are alike houses of representatives. The real difference between them might have been indicated if the upper house had been called the "Federal" house, the lower the "National" house. For the one reflects the fact that Australia is a federation of states; the other reflects the fact that Australia is a nation. In the Senate there are 36 members, 6 for each state; so that all the states are here treated as equally powerful, the smallest and the largest. In the House of Representatives, on the other hand, the states are represented according to their population; New South Wales, at present, sends 27 representatives, Tasmania only 5. The lower house is based on the idea that the will of the majority of Australians ought to prevail;

the upper, on the idea that the larger states must not be allowed to trample on the wishes of the smaller. The lower house assumes the political equality of individual men and women; the upper house assumes the political equality of the states. This will perhaps require a little thinking over.

So far I have spoken as if parliament, as a whole, made the laws; and this appears to be the common belief, for parliament is commonly spoken of as *the legislature*. But this is really somewhat misleading; the laws are not really made by parliament as a whole, but by that small group of members of parliament which we call *the ministry*. It is true that a bill may be introduced by *any* member, but as a matter of fact every important bill is introduced by a member of the ministry; and even a very unimportant bill is not allowed to become law if the ministry is opposed to it. In fact it may be said that the business of parliament is to discuss proposed laws, rather than to make the laws; the ministry is, nowadays, the real legislature. What, then, is the ministry?

The ministry, or *cabinet*,—for it is not necessary for us to distinguish between the two words,—may be described, very briefly, as a small committee consisting of the leaders of that party which has a majority in the lower house. They are chosen in the following way. Suppose the two parties in parliament are called respectively Whigs and Tories. A general election has just been held, and it is found that a majority of the men chosen by the country, as members of the lower house, are Whigs. The Whig party chooses one man as its leader, and this man is immediately "sent for" by the King (or in Australia, by the King's representative) and asked to form a ministry to carry on the government of the country. He submits the names of men who are willing to act with him as ministers; and these are appointed by the King or his representative to govern the country. They are called the ministry, and their leader is called the prime minister. The ministers act together as one body; however they may disagree in private, they publicly take responsibility for one another's actions; or rather, the prime minister is held responsible for the actions of all his fellow-ministers. When ministers disagree on any question, the final decision rests with the prime minister, and if one of his colleagues refuses to accept his decision, he can ask that colleague to resign. Even if all his colleagues resigned, he would still remain prime minister—provided he could get others to fill their places. The ministers are *nominally* appointed by the King or his representative; but they are *really* appointed by the prime minister. (An exception to this rule is the method of the *Labour party* in the Commonwealth parliament. That party, when in power, does not allow the prime minister to choose his colleagues; it chooses them for him. It is too soon to say whether this new plan will turn out a success.) The prime minister is thus the real ruler of the country; and, in a sense, it is he who makes the laws. For, in the first place, the ministry has the very important power of *initiative*; that is, of deciding what bills are to be introduced; no bill can be introduced against the will of the ministry. And in the second place, if the ministry is resolutely determined that a certain bill shall become law, it almost invariably gets its own way; the proposal may be hotly criticised and many shortcomings pointed out, but when it comes to voting, the members of their own party unanimously vote for the ministry; and as this party is in a majority, its vote carries the day. So long as the ministry remains in power—and that means, so long as its party is in a majority in the lower house—it makes the laws, as well as carrying them out.

CHAPTER XXIV.

THE EXECUTIVE.

(a) THE CABINET.

We now see that when people speak of parliament as "the legislature" and of the ministry as "the executive," they speak in a somewhat misleading way. But when people speak, as they commonly do speak, of the ministry as "the government," they speak in a perfectly correct way; for it is the ministry, and not parliament, that governs. It is not the business of parliament to govern; the business of parliament is, as its very name denotes, to parley,—to discuss, to advise, to criticise. The ministry can neither levy a tax, nor undertake any public work, nor make a law, nor amend nor repeal a law, without first submitting its proposal to criticism in parliament. Moreover it is by means of parliament that the people can make and unmake ministries. For if a ministry governs in a way which is disliked by the people, the people have the remedy in their own hands; at the next election, they can return to the lower house a strong majority of the opposite party, the party opposed to the ministry. For a ministry can only continue in office so long as it reflects the opinions of the dominant party in the lower house; when it has no longer a majority at its back, it is bound to resign. What an election really decides is whether the existing ministry shall continue to govern the country, or give place to a new ministry formed of members of the opposite party. Thus the country, through parliament, *controls* the ministry, and can call it to account for its actions. But while a ministry remains in office, it, and not parliament, really governs the country.

We have looked at the ministry in its legislative capacity, as the maker of laws; let us now glance at it in its executive capacity, as carrier-out of laws.

Members of the ministry are, all of them, members of one or other of the two houses of parliament. As you know, this was not always so. Until comparatively recent times, in Britain, the King's ministers were looked upon as personal servants of the King, responsible to the King alone and not to parliament, with which they need have nothing to do. In those days the *executive* was not controlled by parliament. Long after the sovereign had given way in the matter of legislation, long after it had been freely admitted that the King could not make laws without the consent of parliament, it was still held that parliament had nothing to do with the *carrying out* of the laws. When parliament tried to interfere with the executive, it was sternly told to mind its own business. Thus, though every member of the House of Commons might be a Whig, the executive might consist entirely of Tories. But it was felt that a people could not be free or self-governing until it gained control of those who carried out the laws and carried on the general work of government; and the long struggle of the seventeenth century—the struggle which ended with the revolution which cost James II. his throne—may be said to have been a struggle about this question: whether the executive was to be controlled by King or parliament. Even after that revolution, it was some time before people saw the true way to make the executive responsible to parliament. That way is, to make the executive consist of members of parliament—members of the party which is in the majority in the lower house, and which therefore may be presumed to represent a majority of the people. This is the essential feature of the British constitution and of constitutions modelled on the British; it is what distinguishes them, for instance, from a constitution like that of Germany.

The innumerable pieces of work which a modern government is called upon to perform, fall naturally into groups or classes or departments. For instance, all the different duties that are connected with public education may naturally form one department, all the duties connected with the defence of the country form another department. The whole of the work of government is thus split up into several departments, and the ministry consists of heads of departments: that is to say, each minister has a department under his control.

The Commonwealth ministry is smaller than the ministry of any of the states, because the federal constitution did not hand over to the Commonwealth so many branches of government as it left in the hands of the states. The kinds of public work entrusted to the Commonwealth government are indicated in the titles of the Commonwealth ministers. They are: the Treasurer, the Attorney-General, the Postmaster-General, the Ministers of Home Affairs, of External Affairs, of Defence, and of Trade and Customs. The Prime Minister is at the head of the cabinet, but as a general rule he is also the head of one special department; he is usually either Treasurer or Minister of External Affairs. If he does not undertake the control of a department he is said to be "without portfolio," and does not draw the salary of a minister. Mr. Deakin, in 1909, was Prime Minister without portfolio.

At the head of the state cabinet is the Premier—which is just another name for Prime Minister. The other ministers have titles which vary in the various states. In Victoria at the present time the cabinet consists of Premier, Chief Secretary, Treasurer, Attorney-General, Solicitor-General, Ministers of Labour, Water-Supply, Agriculture, Public Health, Public Works, Lands, Education, Railways, Mines and Forests. But there is not necessarily a separate Minister for each of these departments: one man may have two or three

THE FEDERAL PARLIAMENT IN SESSION.

departments under his control. For instance, at present (1912) the Premier of Victoria is also Chief Secretary and Minister of Labour; the Minister of Water-Supply is also the Minister of Agriculture; and so on. But a minister is not allowed to draw a double salary because he directs two departments.

If you go back and look carefully over those lists of ministers, you will be able to gain a fair idea of the kinds of work done by the Commonwealth and State governments respectively. You will notice that the two lists have certain titles in common. For instance, in both Commonwealth and State cabinets there must be a Treasurer, who deals with money matters—taxation, revenue and expenditure; and an Attorney-General, who is the legal adviser of the government, and a link between the executive and the judiciary. Moreover, the federal Minister of Home Affairs corresponds pretty closely with the State Chief Secretary (or Colonial Secretary, as he is called in some states); this minister may be described as dealing with all matters which do not fall under any of the other departments. But there is no Minister of Defence in the state cabinet, because by the federal constitution the states have nothing to do with questions of defence. And there is no Minister of Education in the federal cabinet, because education was not one of the matters handed over by the states to the Commonwealth.

(b) THE CIVIL SERVICE.

"It is not the business of a Cabinet Minister to work his department. His business is to see that it is properly worked."[10] A minister undertakes to see that certain of the duties of government are performed; but whether he can carry out his undertaking depends on the instru-

10   Sir George Cornewall Lewis.

ments he has at his disposal. These instruments are the men and women permanently employed in the doing of public work. It is by their means alone that a minister is enabled to give effect to the will of the people. For instance, it may be the wish of the people that a good education be given to every child in their state. It is the duty of the Minister of Education to see that this is done; but he is quite powerless in the matter unless he has at his command an army of trained, skilful, and conscientious teachers. A Minister of Railways, however clever, cannot provide us with a good railway system unless he can find men who will build locomotives and trucks and car-riages, men who will build bridges and lay down lines, navvies, and porters, and guards, and station-masters, and signal-men, and many more. And so it is with every department of government; whether its work is ill or well done depends, not on the minister, but on the officers and men who actually do the work. These officers and men are called Civil Servants.

The Minister is the *parliamentary head* of his department; but the department needs also a *permanent head*. The difference between these two is not merely the difference between a commander-in-chief and his second-in-command. It is rather the difference between the amateur and the expert, between the layman and the professional. The minister has not as a rule any professional knowledge of the matters with which he deals; nor need he have. He may be at the head of his department for a few years only, or even only a few months. When the ministry to which he belongs is beaten, he must resign with the other ministers. The permanent head, on the other hand, keeps his place while ministers come and go; the work of his depart-ment has been the study of his lifetime; he is fitted for his duties by long experience and a technical training. The minister lays down the broad lines on which the department is to be worked; but as a rule he knows little about the technical details. He may be an excellent Minister of Railways, without knowing anything whatever about the building of a locomotive. He is responsible to parliament for the work his department does. It is his part, therefore, to say what shall be done; but he must trust the permanent head to say *how* it can be done. Under the permanent head, and taking their orders from him, are officers of various ranks, each of them equipped with technical knowledge of his own branch of the work. And under the officers are the rank and file of the men; some of them, too, require a long technical training; others, such as navvies, require little more than physical strength and endurance. But all alike, officers and men, must do their work well and faithfully if the department is to be worked satisfactorily.

A highly important point in our constitution is that the civil servants are independent of political parties. They are not appointed, nor promoted, nor dismissed, by the ministry, but by an independent authority, consisting of one or more persons appointed for the purpose. And as the civil servant has nothing either to hope or fear from any particular ministry, so should he be equally willing to serve any ministry. It is his duty to serve one minister as loyally as he serves another, though he may disagree with the views of one and think the other's views are right. The minister represents, for him, the people's will; and his duty is to carry out the will of the people to the best of his ability.

CHAPTER XXV.

THE POWER OF PARLIAMENT.

Writers on the British Constitution often use the phrase "the Sovereignty of parliament," or "the omnipotence of parliament"; and while it is true that the real sovereignty rests with the people, which can make and unmake parliaments, yet it is also true that, in Britain, there is a very real sense in which parliament is omnipotent. Let us see where Australia differs from Britain in this respect.

In Britain, when the nation has chosen a parliament, it makes over its sovereignty to that parliament. There is no law which parliament cannot make; there is no law which parliament cannot repeal or unmake. You may say that it is bound to govern according to the British constitution, but this means nothing, because parliament has the power of altering the constitution, and has often exercised that power. So lately as in 1911 it made a fundamental change in the constitution, by limiting in certain ways the powers of the House of Lords. In 1716 parliament decreed that it should sit for seven years instead of three; obviously, if it could do that, it could also have decreed that it should sit permanently, and that there should be no more elections. Doubtless, if it had done that, it would have stirred up immediate rebellion; but there would have been nothing illegal in its action, because parliament cannot do anything illegal—it can unmake any law. In this sense it is omnipotent.

But what about the power of the King? The result of the great struggles of the seventeenth and eighteenth centuries is that the power of the Crown, as someone has said, has been changed into influence; the King may exercise a powerful influence on the actions of parliament, but he no longer possesses any real power to interfere with parliament's decisions. There are many words and phrases still in use which would lead a foreigner to think that the King was an absolute monarch; but such words and phrases no longer correspond with reality; they are like the *b* in *doubt* and the *k* in *knave*—survivals of an earlier time, when they had a real meaning. "Le Roy le veult"—the formula in which the King's assent is still given to an act of parliament—is a survival of the time when Norman French was spoken in the English parliament, and when acts of parliament were petitions to the King. If you look at an act of parliament in one of our Australian states, Victoria, for instance, you will see that it begins with the words: *"Be it enacted by the King's Most Excellent Majesty by and with the advice and consent of the Legislative Council and Legislative Assembly of Victoria in this present Parliament assembled and by the authority of the same,"*—and this is a copy of the formula with which all British acts of parliament commence. But parliament does not really *advise* the King to take a certain course of action; it decides to take that course, and though the King's assent is still required, it is always given as a matter of course; it is a mere formality. The King is no longer, in reality, what he is still often called—the head of the executive; the head of the executive is the Prime Minister.

We may note in passing, that though the sovereign power has been wrested from the nominal Sovereign, yet the phrase, "loyalty to the King," is still full of real meaning. We are loyal to the King because he is the symbol of the national unity, a symbol of the enduring majesty of the British Empire. Parliaments may come and go, ministries may rise and fall, one party may triumph over the other and be triumphed over in its turn; but, above and beyond all changes of ministry and tides of party, the King remains. He is thus the symbol of the nation itself, which abides through all change; and loyalty to the King means loyalty to the Empire of which he is the chief citizen and servant.

The parliaments of the Australian states are, like the British parliament, omnipotent in the sense that they have the power of altering their own constitutions; but in another sense their power is limited, and that in two ways. In the first place, they must do nothing which conflicts with the act of the British parliament which called them into being. The Governor, who is called the King's representative, but who is really, in this matter, the representative of the British ministry, may withhold the royal assent from an act of one of these parliaments, thus preventing it from becoming law, until it has been considered by the King—that is, by the British cabinet; and that cabinet may refuse to allow it to become law. In the second place, the power of a state parliament is limited by the fact that, as we have seen, certain matters have been handed over by the states to the Commonwealth, and the state parliament must not meddle in these matters.

The Commonwealth parliament has far more strictly limited powers. To begin with, though it has a far wider power than a state parliament in a geographical sense—though it is powerful throughout *all* the states—yet it is powerful in a far smaller number of matters. For the Commonwealth constitution gives it power in certain definite matters, and in all other matters it leaves the power to the separate states; therefore it is evident that a state parliament has power to legislate over an immeasurably wider range of subjects than the Commonwealth parliament can.

In the second place, the state parliament, as we have seen, can alter its own constitution; the Commonwealth parliament cannot alter the constitution of Australia—at least, it cannot do so without asking permission from the people of Australia. Everyone who has a vote for the Commonwealth parliament, every Australian elector, must be given the opportunity of answering the question—which is printed on small slips of paper—"do you, or do you not, approve of the proposed alteration?" And before the alteration can be made, there must not merely be a majority of electors in favour of it, but majorities of electors *in a majority of the states*. This is called the *referendum*; it is a device whereby parliament is prevented from changing the constitution of the Commonwealth without a direct appeal to the people.

Moreover, the Commonwealth parliament has strictly limited powers in this sense, that it is rigidly bound by the constitution, and that its actions, if they seem to go beyond the constitution, may be challenged in a court of law. This is a thing unheard of in Britain; for there, as we have seen, there is no law which parliament cannot make; and when a law is once made, the law-courts are bound to uphold it. But it has happened several times already in the Commonwealth, that parliament has passed a law which the High Court of Australia has afterwards declared to be unconstitutional; the parliament, that is, is declared to have gone beyond its powers, and the supposed law is therefore no law at all. The chief duty of the High Court is to act as *guardian of the constitution*—to see that the Commonwealth parliament does only those things which by the constitution it is permitted to do.

CHAPTER XXVI.

THE JUDICIARY.

The last of the three organs of government is not the least important of them; rather, it is the most important of all. For, even in a country where the Legislature makes the wisest and fairest laws and where the Executive does its work with the greatest possible efficiency, there will be very little genuine liberty and very little real justice if the Judiciary is not strong enough to protect those who cannot protect themselves, and to punish offenders against the law. When a dispute occurs between two citizens, we need someone to settle it by saying what the law is, and by insisting that the law be obeyed. When one man has wronged another, we need someone to right the wrong. When a man is accused of a crime, we need someone to find out whether he has really committed the crime, and, if he has, to say what punishment the law prescribes for him. In other words, we need some kind of machinery to interpret the law, and to apply it to particular cases; and this machinery is called the Judiciary.

This statement suggests a distinction which is very important: the distinction between Civil and Criminal Justice. Civil justice is concerned with *wrongs* done by one citizen to another; the business of the judiciary is to *remedy* that wrong. Criminal justice is concerned with *crimes*, which are wrongs done to the whole community; the business of the judiciary is to *punish* the wrongdoer. In a civil case, there may be no evil intention; two men may have a dispute about the ownership of a piece of land, and each may honestly believe himself to be the owner; they take the question to the law-courts to have it settled for them. Or there may be no dispute about the facts: Smith may owe Brown a sum of money and refuse to pay it; Brown brings a *law-suit* against Smith, and the law-court forces Smith to pay the money. It does not punish him for not having paid it, because he has not committed a crime; but he has wronged another, and the law-court insists that he shall make restitution. Of course there is no clear-cut distinction between a wrong and a crime; a wrong may be a crime, and a crime is generally a wrong done to somebody. For instance, when A forges B's signature to a cheque, he has done a wrong to B in trying to cheat him out of some money, and he has also, in forging a signature, committed a very serious crime. Still, in the main the distinction holds: in a civil case, the law provides a remedy; in a criminal case, the law provides a punishment. In a civil case, there is always a *plaintiff*, who asserts that he has been wronged, and a *defendant*, who is accused of having wronged the plaintiff. In a criminal case, there is no plaintiff and there is a defendant; or rather, society is really the plaintiff; and the defendant—who is called "the accused"—is held to have done a wrong to the whole community by breaking its laws.

Another way of putting the difference is this: in a civil case, one man calls upon the law to help him against another man; and unless he so calls, the law will not help him. Thus, A may owe B a thousand pounds, or a hundred thousand pounds, and refuse to pay; unless B chooses to "take proceedings" against A in a law-court, the law-courts will not interfere; it is B's own business, and he may do as he likes about it. But if A has committed a murder, and B knows it, then B is not given any choice in the matter. It is not *his* business this time—it is the business of the whole community; and if he conceals his knowledge of the crime, he is himself committing a crime. For a murder is not a private matter between one citizen and another; it is not merely a wrong done by one citizen to another; it is a blow struck at the well-being of society, and society (through its judiciary) does its utmost to bring the criminal to justice, that he may be punished in such a way as is most likely to prevent such crimes in the future.

The Judiciary deals with both civil and criminal cases by means of *law-courts* of various kinds, from the lowest to the highest. First there are the Courts of Petty Sessions, or Police Courts as they are commonly called, presided over by magistrates or justices of the peace. The powers of these courts are strictly limited, but the limitations are different in the different states; roughly speaking, we may say that they can only deal with civil cases in which the amount at stake does not exceed £50, and with criminal cases in which the penalty is not greater than six months' imprisonment. (In Victoria, the magistrates have the power of imposing a sentence up to two years for certain offences, but this power is very rarely exercised.) As a rule, these courts deal with the less important civil cases and with petty offences against the law. A person accused of a *serious* crime is *first* brought before one of these lower courts, which has the power of determining whether there is any evidence against him; if there is, the court sends him up to a higher court to be tried. Above the police courts are the County Courts, presided over, not by magistrates, but by judges—"County court judges"— who have power to decide in civil cases in which the amount in dispute is not more than £500. County courts do not deal with criminal cases. The highest court, in each state, is the Supreme Court, which is presided over by one of the supreme court judges. All the most important cases, both civil and criminal, are tried by the Supreme Court.

Besides the law-courts of the various states, there is a federal court—the High Court of Australia; consisting, at present, of a Chief Justice and four other judges. So far, the most important duties of the High Court have been to hear appeals against the decisions of the state courts, and to act as guardians of the Commonwealth constitution, in the manner described elsewhere[11].

It would take too much space if I attempted to tell you in detail how each of these courts does its work. But all the courts are open to the public, and anyone who is interested may go and see for himself how our judiciary performs its important tasks. An hour spent in one of the courts will tell you more about the matter than you could learn from many pages of description. At the same time, you ought to understand certain important principles underlying the administration of justice in our country. The first thing to notice is—*the independence of the judges*. This is an important safeguard of our liberties, and it had to be fought for; there was a time when the judges were servants of the monarch, liable to be dismissed from their posts if they did not decide cases in accordance with his wish. Richard II., during his brief career as a tyrant, threatened the judges with dire penalties if they declined to give the verdict he wished them to give; and James I. dismissed Chief Justice Coke because he declared that a royal proclamation could not alter the law of the land. The complete independence of the judges was not secured until the Act of Settlement (in 1701) declared that no judge could be removed except by the will of both houses of Parliament. That means that our judges cannot be interfered with by the King, the Prime Minister, or anyone else, unless Parliament as a whole declares him unfit for his duties. He is placed in a position where he can fearlessly and impartially declare the law of the land.

The second thing to note is that, under the British system, a man accused of a serious crime is not tried by a judge alone, but by a judge assisted by a jury of twelve men, chosen by lot. "Trial by Jury" is one of the most famous of British institutions, and it has always

11   See Chapter 25, p. 198.

been looked upon as one of the greatest bulwarks of personal liberty that any nation has devised. It may seem at first sight a strange thing that justice should be administered by twelve ordinary citizens, who may know nothing whatever about the law, instead of by the judge, a trained lawyer of great skill and long experience. But the jury does not need to know anything of the law, because its duty is simply to judge of the *facts* of the case. Did A, as a matter of fact, murder B, or did he not? Is the evidence sufficient to show that he committed the crime, or is it insufficient? When the jury has declared that the prisoner is guilty, or not guilty, of the crime of which he is accused, its task is ended; it has nothing to do with the law, but only with the facts of the case. The judge's duty is to see that the trial is conducted properly, and also to make it perfectly clear to the jury on what questions of fact they must decide; and it is his duty to say, if the prisoner is found guilty, what punishment the law prescribes; but he must not attempt to persuade the jury to return a verdict of "guilty" or "not guilty," however strong his own opinion may be. The jury's verdict must be unanimous. That is to say, before anyone can be punished for a crime, twelve jurors must have agreed that he is guilty of that crime. It is not necessary to point out how this system protects our liberties, what a safeguard it is against tyranny and unfairness. Doubtless the jury system has enabled great numbers of guilty persons to escape from justice; but this should not be allowed to weigh against the far more important fact, that it has saved many thousands of innocent persons from injustice.

PART IV.
CITIZENSHIP.

CHAPTER XXVII.

LIBERTY.

We must now return to a question raised in an earlier chapter—the question of Government versus Liberty. As we have surveyed the principal activities of government, at every step we have found compulsion and restraint. Government compels us to pay taxes; it compels everyone to send his children to school; it compels the orchardist to spray his apple-trees; it compels boys to drill and shoot; it restrains the butcher from selling tainted meat; it restrains the mine-owner from employing children in his mine; it restrains the careless person from having a filthy back-yard; and so on. Where,—it may be asked,—where, amid all these compulsions and restraints, is there room for liberty, which means freedom to do as we please, without let or hindrance? Government would seem to be just a splendid machine for destroying liberty.

To understand that this is not so, and that government, instead of being the enemy of liberty, is really the best friend liberty has, you will have to stop and ask yourself whether you are quite sure what liberty really means.

In the first place, *liberty does not mean mere freedom from restraint.* If it did, then liberty would be forever impossible to human beings; his very nature imposes innumerable restraints on a man. The nature of his body, for instance, restrains him; he cannot see through a brick wall, or jump over Bass's Strait, or do without sleep for a year, or take off his head when it aches and put it back when it is better; his body is so made that he can do none of these things. And the nature of his mind restrains him; we speak of freedom of thought, but no-one can think, however hard he tries to, that two and two make five, or that black is white, or that a straight line is not the shortest distance between any two points. In the same way, his nature as a social being restrains him; the fact that he is a member of society restrains him from doing things which would make society impossible. Men claim liberty as a sacred right; but no sane man claims, as a right, the freedom to do things that would interfere with the general welfare. If liberty meant that kind of freedom, then of course it would be the sacred duty of society to do away with liberty. But that was not the kind of freedom for which our fathers fought and bled.

Their fight for liberty was, indeed, a fight against restraints, but it was not against restraints in general; they did not say that the murderer must not be restrained from murdering, or the robber from robbing. They fought against unjust, unwise, or unnecessary restraints; against restraints imposed by the will of one man (a king) or a body of powerful men; against all restraints except such as the welfare of the whole people required. But they did not fight against restraints in general, for that would have been to fight against government, against order; and they knew that he who fights against order fights against liberty. For without order, the strongest and the wickedest would always prevail, and the rest would be slaves to them.

Liberty—the only liberty worth fighting for—should be thought of, not as freedom *from*, but as freedom *to*; not freedom from this or that restraint, but freedom to do this or that thing that is worth doing. Not freedom to do whatever one pleases; a drunkard may please to drink too much, and may be free to do it, but he has no real liberty; no man is more of a slave than he. But freedom to do what our best self tells us we ought to do—freedom to make the best of our bodies and minds—freedom to live the very finest kind of life possible to our nature—that is liberty. And if we use the word in that sense, then we shall find that government is in truth the best friend of liberty.

For *social* liberty—the kind of liberty which a society as a whole can seek to gain—is not consistent with liberty in the negative sense, in the sense of freedom from restraint. The liberty of the whole society can only be secured by putting restraints on individuals; and you will find that, in a well-governed country, when a restraint is put on someone's liberty to do as he pleases, it is in order to help someone else to escape from slavery. A very obvious instance has already been given: in the early nineteenth century, it becomes quite plain that the unrestrained liberty of the factory owner meant the practical enslavement of multitudes of children. Again, the unrestrained liberty of parents to do as they liked with their children had to be interfered with in the interests of the children themselves; they, too, had a claim to liberty. So long as liberty means only freedom from restraint, then one man's liberty means another man's bondage. Now the fundamental principle of democracy is that no-one ought to be kept in bondage in order that another may be free to do as he pleases; that liberty is the birthright of all alike; and that government must put restraints on the liberty of some, in order that it may secure the largest measure of liberty to all.

But look on liberty as a positive thing,—as freedom to do, to be, to enjoy, to understand,—and you will find that, in innumerable ways, government sets us free. The measure of a man's liberty is the measure of his opportunities; and a modern civilized man, living under a government which imposes numerous and elaborate rules upon him, has a thousandfold more opportunities than a primitive savage has or can have. Government, to take a simple instance, compels us to be educated, and by so doing it gives us opportunities to do and to enjoy and to understand things of which the ignorant savage does not dream. You will not need to search very long to find many other ways in which government helps us to lead a fuller, a more varied, and a happier life than would otherwise be possible to us. The aim of the best government is to make the best kind of life possible to all. It seeks the common good; and therefore it grants only such liberties as do not conflict with the common good. But, it may be asked, could not the common good be secured without any liberty being granted at all to the governed? Might not a wise and benevolent despot, ruling over a nation of slaves, do more for their well-being than liberty could ever do? No; because liberty is itself an indispensable part of the general well-being, an essential condition of the best kind of life; that is the principle underlying democratic government. That is why men have striven that the right of voting might be extended to all grown-up citizens. For the right to vote, unimportant as it may seem, and little as it may appear to benefit its possessor, is yet a part of liberty; it is a gateway by which we enter into the larger life of our country; it is an opportunity for playing a part, however humble, in public affairs; nor can anyone be called completely free to whom this opportunity is denied.

But if individual liberty is a priceless part of our well-being, and if government interferes, as it often does, with individual liberty in order to secure the general well-being, how are we to reconcile the apparent contradiction?

If someone told you that you must not drink kerosene, would you call that an interference with your liberty? "Certainly not," you will say; "who wants to drink kerosene?" And suppose someone told you to eat when you were hungry, would you call that an infringement of your liberty? "Why, no; it is just what I want to do." So, then, you do not feel that your liberty is interfered with, if you are only restrained from doing what you have no desire to do, and if you are only compelled to do what you are yourself eager to do? If that be so, let us examine the restraints and compulsions put upon us by government, and see whether they are real interferences with liberty.

INFANTS' ROOM IN A SOUTH AUSTRALIAN SCHOOL.

Take compulsory education. If one hates learning, one feels this to be a hardship; but if one is eager above all things for knowledge and understanding, if one is earnestly longing to be educated, then the fact that education is compulsory never for a moment seems to be an interference with liberty. So with military service; if you have no love for your country, or if you do not understand her need of defenders, you will probably think drill a grievous hardship; but if you do understand, and if you so love your country that you can accept, eagerly and rejoicingly, any opportunity of serving her, then you will not feel this to be any violation of your personal liberty. You do not feel that your liberty is interfered with unless you are forced to act, or abstain from acting, *against your will*; the consenting will is the essence of liberty. In so far as your will consents to the law,—in so far, that is, as you obey the law eagerly and gladly,—you are serving, not a harsh tyrant, but a master "whose service is perfect Freedom."

If this be so, it follows that the good citizen of a well-governed country is the only person who can enjoy true liberty. For the law, in a well-governed country, only restrains us from doing those things which, if we are good citizens, we have no wish to do. Government, in a well-governed country, only compels us to do things which, if we are good citizens, we should eagerly desire to do even if there were no compulsion. In fact, a well-governed country may be defined as a country in which the best citizens have the fullest measure of liberty; for good government is only the carrying out of the will of the best citizens.

Is Australia a well-governed country? To answer that question, you have to examine your daily life, and consider what sort of things you are forbidden to do and what sort of things you are compelled to do. And if you think of something that you would like to do but which government restrains you from doing, you must ask yourself— "Would I wish to do this, if I were a good citizen,—that is, if I had a keen regard for the welfare of the community as a whole? Would it be good for the community as a whole if people were allowed to do this?" And you will soon discover that there are very, very few things which government forbids you to do which are not things that a good citizen would of his own accord abstain from doing.

Consider, in like manner, the things government compels you to do; and ask yourself, fairly and honestly, whether they are not just the things that your conscience tells you you ought to do; you will find that, with very few exceptions, they are.

There may be exceptions; for in no country in the world are the laws perfect, and the best government has its defects. And that is why self-government is so essential a part of liberty. In so far as you have to obey a law which your conscience tells you is unjust, in so far as you are compelled to do something which you know to be not in the best interests of the community, just to that extent you are not free. But the member of a self-governing society knows that the laws he obeys are laws which society itself has made, and can unmake. By your vote, and still more by influencing public opinion and so by affecting the votes of other people, you can help to remedy the defect, and by so doing to increase the measure of liberty enjoyed by you and your fellow-citizens.

CHAPTER XXVIII.

LAW.

We have heard a great deal about our forefathers' heroic struggles for liberty; it is rather startling, when we come to read the history of Britain, to find that what they really fought for was, most often, not liberty but Law. Take, for instance, the great struggle of the seventeenth century, the struggle which cost one of the Stuarts his life and another his throne; over and over again you find Parliament remonstrating with the sovereign, not for enforcing harsh laws, but for going outside the laws, for acting illegally. The Stuart kings seemed fatally incapable of abiding by the great principle of the British constitution, that the King is bound to govern in accordance with the laws of his realm; and their failure to accept this ancient rule brought civil war to Britain. The great rebellion of that century was not a rebellion against the law; it was a rising in defence of the law. And why were men willing to shed their blood in defence of the law? Because they were wise enough to know that law is the great safeguard of personal liberty; because they knew that *the rule of law is the only thing that can save us from the rule of men.* Our liberty is never safe unless the law stands, sacred and inviolable, supreme over the arbitrary will of tyrants, high above the quarrels of individual men, ruling with steady impartiality over high and low, rich and poor, strong and weak alike. Perhaps this is the most striking feature of the British constitution—the supremacy of law. At the very roots of that constitution are to be found two propositions:

(1) That no man is punishable, in body or in goods, except after a distinct breach of the law, proved against him in a fair trial before the ordinary courts of the law.

(2) That all men are equal before the law.

Though these two rules have been broken again and again, by kings and by the ministers of kings, and though they have often required to be re-asserted, they have been recognised from the very earliest times to be a fundamental part of the British constitution.

Consider that first proposition, and ask what chance personal liberty has in a country where it is unknown. In France before the Revolution, for instance, if you were an influential person, you could get from the government what was called a *lettre de cachet*, by means of which you could have any person you disliked shut up for an indefinite number of years in some terrible prison, such as the infamous *Bastille*; and of course the King, and the King's ministers, continually used this power. A man might be arrested and imprisoned for life without any trial, and without even knowing whom he had offended, or how. This went on until the French people abhorred the very name of the Bastille, and at last they rose and destroyed it, and went on to destroy the system of government under which such horrors had been possible.

But we do not need to go to France for an example. Many instances of imprisonment without trial could be quoted from British history; there have been times when it was quite common for an English sovereign to send to prison those who had offended him, or those of whom he was afraid. "To none will we deny justice," said King John in the Great Charter that was wrung from him; but that Charter was often violated. In Charles I.'s time, for instance, men were thrown into prison for refusing to pay a tax which the King had (illegally) imposed on them; they appealed in vain to the clause of the Great Charter which declared that "no man shall be imprisoned except by the legal judgment of his peers or by the law of the land"; in vain they claimed the right to know at least for what breach of the law they were kept in prison. Such a thing could not happen today in any part of the British Empire, because no-one now dares to question the firmly established principle, that a man cannot be imprisoned except after having been proved to have broken the law.

"To none will we *delay* justice," said King John; and this, too, was a very important promise, a promise often made and often broken. Long after King John's time, we find justice being grievously delayed; we hear of a man lying in prison for years awaiting his trial. A guarantee of personal liberty was at last secured by the nation in the great *Habeas Corpus Act of 1679*, which provides that no man shall be kept in prison untried.

"To none will we sell justice" was another promise made in the Great Charter; but centuries later we still find justice being bought and sold. We find the government using arbitrary imprisonment as a means of extorting money; rich offenders against the law using their wealth to save them from justice; poor men, wronged by the rich, unable to obtain redress, just because they were poor. But it was always recognized that this was a violation of the spirit of our laws; and nowadays it is a firmly established principle, that justice must not swerve from its course for all the wealth of all the millionaires; and to offer a bribe to a judge, or to try to buy the good-will of a jury, is regarded as a heinous offence.

It is quite plain, then, that law is the great protector of our liberty; that the rule of law saves us from the rule of men; that so long as we cannot legally be imprisoned or made to suffer in person or property unless we have broken the law, we are safe from the arbitrary tyranny of powerful men. Moreover, every man is held to be innocent until he has been proved to be guilty; and that means that no-one can be punished except after a fair trial in one of the *ordinary* courts of justice. In the seventeenth century various *extraordinary* courts—such as the Court of Star Chamber and the High Commission Court—unjustly and tyrannically oppressed and deprived of their liberty many innocent persons. Perhaps the most dangerous feature of these extraordinary tribunals was their secrecy. The only courts of justice known to us today are open to the public; what takes place in them is reported in our newspapers; nothing is hidden from the daylight, everything is open and above-board. This is a most precious guarantee against oppression.

Vitally important, also, is the principle that "all men are equal before the law." The law is impartial. Justice is represented, in statues, as blindfolded; she takes no account of differences of rank or class. No man is so rich or so powerful that he can break the law with impunity; no man is so poor or so humble that the law will not protect him. Every man is subject to the ordinary law of the land; every man who breaks the law, however exalted his position may be, must pay the penalty which law prescribes. Even Parliament is subject to the law; Parliament may abolish a law, but until it is abolished, even Parliament must obey it. Even the Cabinet Ministers are responsible before the courts of law; and if a cabinet minister, either as a private citizen or in his public capacity as a minister, does us a wrong, we can prosecute him in the ordinary courts and force him to pay the penalty for his breach of the law. Thus the law protects us against the possible tyranny of those in power.

It protects us, too, against the tyranny of the majority—perhaps the most dangerous enemy that liberty, in democratic countries, has to fight against. In some of the states of America, as we have noticed, it sometimes happens that a man has incurred so much popular indignation that the crowd "takes the law into its own hands," and punishes him, even with death, without any trial at all. According to our ideas, this is simply murder, and we would regard it as the duty of the law to put forth all its powers in defence of such a man, no matter what crime he might be accused of having committed. Even in our own country, and especially in times of excitement, a man who has made himself unpopular by his opinions or his actions may be in danger of suffering violence at the hands of a hostile majority. The law cannot prevent him from suffering, in many ways, for his unpopularity; but it can at least protect him from violence. It says—"No: this man has a perfect right to his own opinions, and to utter them; he has a perfect right to do as he thinks right, so long as he does not act illegally; *you*, at any rate, shall not touch him—or, if you do, you shall pay the penalty." And as a matter of fact, a crowd, however excited and angry it may be, very seldom, in our country, proceeds to acts of violence; because we as a people have inherited, along with other British traditions, a great respect for law.

It is the duty of a citizen to hold the law sacred, and to obey it with the most scrupulous exactness, and to do all he can to help those whose work it is to enforce the law. We ought to obey a law even when we disapprove of it. We may do all in our power to get a law altered or abolished, but while it is the law we are bound to abide by it. Because it is only by reverence for the law that the inestimable blessing of liberty has been gained for us, and it is only by our own reverence for the law that we shall preserve that blessing.

CHAPTER XXIX.

EQUALITY.

Democracy is sometimes said to be founded on the principle of equality; on the belief, that is, that all men are by nature equal. We can understand, and sympathize with, the feelings of the Frenchmen who first made this assertion; everywhere around them they saw oppression and injustice, terrible abuse of power, and hopeless misery, all springing, as they thought, from artificial inequalities, inequalities of power and wealth. On the one hand they saw a powerful nobleman, rich, unscrupulous, selfish, trampling under foot the lives of his social inferiors; on the other hand they saw a starving peasant, poor, down-trodden, condemned to a life of hopeless drudgery. "Look at these two men," they said, "is there any reason in nature for the wide difference in their fates? There is none; the nobleman is not by nature one whit better, or wiser, or stronger than the peasant. If he is stronger and cleverer *now*, that is due to his upbringing, not to any gifts of nature. If the two had been changed in their cradles, if the noble had been brought up in the peasant's hut and the peasant in the nobleman's castle, then the peasant would now be the strong and unscrupulous noble, and the other would now be the spiritless and down-trodden drudge. Nature made them equal; it is the artificial arrangements of society that have brought about the tremendous difference between them. Therefore the arrangements of society are defective, and must be changed." So they preached, these Frenchmen; and the result was the French Revolution, the greatest attempt that has ever been made to change the whole social fabric of a nation.

And yet it would be a pity if democracy had no better foundation than the doctrine that nature made all men equal; for if we take that statement strictly, it is meaningless, and if we take it less strictly, it is quite untrue. It is meaningless to talk of men as equal, because equality is a mathematical idea; you can say that two lines are equal, or that two weights are equal, or that two areas are equal, but you cannot say that two men are equal; you cannot weigh intelligence in the scales, or measure goodness with a tape. When you say that all men are by nature equal, you really mean that all are by nature alike; and you have no sooner said this than you see it to be untrue. Do you think that if you had been brought up exactly as Nero was, you would be exactly like Nero; or that if I had been brought up exactly as Shakespeare was, I could have written Shakespeare's plays? No, nature does not make all men alike; it would be far nearer the truth to say that nature never makes two men alike. No matter how much alike two men may seem, if you knew them better you would find great differences between them,—deep-seated differences, differences for which nature is responsible.

Yet, as we have seen, it has been believed for many centuries that the law ought to treat all men as equal. Is there any justification for treating all men as equal, when all men are obviously *not* equal? There is; the doctrine of equality has a solid foundation; it is founded on the rock of our common humanity. We say that the law ought to treat all men as equal, just because they are men; they are all alike human beings; and, as human beings, though they may differ in certain respects, the respects in which they resemble one another are more numerous still. Because we are human beings, we have the capacity for love and hatred, for hope and fear, for heroism and cowardice, for joy and sorrow. Our minds are governed by the same laws; bad reasoning in London is bad reasoning in Pekin.

Human beings have the capacity for choosing between right and wrong, between doing and neglecting their duty; this is perhaps the great difference between man and the lower animals. We say that a human being *ought* or ought not to act in a certain way; we do not use the word *ought* about dogs and horses. It is just because all men are alike capable of choosing between right and wrong, and because all men are capable of suffering, of being hurt by the wrongdoing of others, that the idea of *justice* arises; for justice is founded on the idea of equality. If a father, for instance, treats one son harshly and another gently when both have committed the same offence, we say that he is acting u*nfairly or unjustly*. The idea of law is perfect fairness; and therefore law must treat all *as if* they were exactly alike.

But, you may say, no two men are exactly alike even in their power of distinguishing right from wrong; and one man suffers more intensely than another would from the same blow; surely we ought to take account of these differences? So perhaps we ought, if we could see into one another's hearts; if there were anyone wise enough to know exactly how much of the sense of duty is in one man's mind, or how much pain another man is suffering. But since we cannot do this, the only just way is to treat all men as if they were exactly alike.

But is there no other field, besides this of the law, in which all men should be treated as if they were exactly alike? We, in Australia, have decided that there is; that equality before the law must be followed by *political equality*. Every grown-up person has a vote for the Commonwealth Parliament; no-one has more than one vote; all grown-up people have exactly equal power in choosing representatives. Here we are on disputed ground; many persons who believe in equality before the law do not believe in political equality; for here the differences between men are glaringly obvious, and it seems at first sight ridiculous that a stupid and thoughtless person should have just as much say in governing the country as a wise and far-seeing person who has devoted years to the study of political questions. But, here again, how are you going to measure political capacity, the capacity for choosing fit men to rule? How are you going to determine that A's wisdom is exactly four times as much as B's, so that A shall have four votes to B's one? How are you going to find out that C is unfit to have a vote at all? There is no way—no way that does not lead to tyranny and injustice. Moreover, we believe that the only way to give a man political capacity is to give him political responsibility. The only way to teach anyone to use a vote is to give him a vote to use.

Can we carry this principle of equality with us into *economic* questions—questions of wealth, of the rewards of labour? This is far too complicated a problem to be discussed here; but there are one or two points to which I may draw your attention.

However we may dispute about men's natural equality or inequality, there can be no dispute about the fact of men's inequality of fortune. Even in countries where equality before the law and political equality are firmly established, the most stupendous inequality in the matter of wealth continues to exist. It is less stupendous in Australia than in some other countries; but even in Australia there are millionaires and paupers living side by side, and, between these two extremes, every degree of wealth and poverty. Now we need not here consider the questions, whether all this inequality of wealth ought to be swept away as political inequality was swept away; whether this would be a happier country if all men had exactly equal yearly incomes; whether such a state of things could be brought about, and whether, if it were brought about, it could be maintained even for a single week. All we need ask ourselves is, whether the present inequality is consistent with justice. Justice does not, it would seem, demand equality of wealth; justice rather demands inequality— demands that the industrious man shall receive the due reward of his industry, and that the idle man shall suffer for his idleness. At any rate, the good citizen need not desire anything so remote and so questionable as the equal distribution of wealth; what he is bound to desire with all his heart is the *just* distribution of wealth. He is bound to ask himself whether our present distribution of wealth is founded on *justice*.

Many arguments for inequality of wealth might be brought forward; many reasons might be given why one man should be rich and another poor; but none of them will explain or justify our present inequality. It might be said, for instance, that men must always be paid according to their intelligence; that ability must always command a high price; that the man capable of governing a country must always be paid enormously higher wages than the man who is only capable of using pick and shovel. Whether that be a just principle or not, at any rate it is not the principle of our present distribution; we all know that the richest people are not the ablest, and there seems no reason to doubt that there is just as much natural intelligence among the poor as among the rich. Again, it might be said that a man should be paid according to the amount of work he does; that wealth should be the reward of industry, quite apart from ability. Obviously *that* is not our principle; look around you, and you will find among the poorest people men who toil incessantly, and among the richest people men who have never really worked in their lives. Again, it has been urged that men who do the most difficult and unpleasant work of the world should, in fairness, be paid the highest wage. That, of course, is almost exactly the reverse of our present principle; on the whole, we find that those who do the most unpleasant kind of work are the most poorly paid. We might suggest half-a-dozen other possible principles, and none of them would fit the facts as we know them. We are tempted to conclude, in despair, that wealth, among us, is distributed on no principle at all; that it is a matter of *chance*; that, in the main, the size of a man's share of this world's goods depends on the class into which he has chanced to be born.

It is impossible to speak here of the various plans that have been proposed for remedying the defects of our present distribution of wealth; it is enough to have pointed out that some remedy is required. Few will deny that the present state of things is profoundly unsatisfactory. To use the old phrase once more, the aim of society, through its machinery of government, is to throw open to every citizen a gateway to the best and noblest kind of life; or, in other words, to promote the common welfare. Now material prosperity is not, and must never be mistaken for, true welfare; to put more money in his purse is not necessarily to add to a man's welfare. But a certain measure of material prosperity is necessary to true welfare; a man must be able to face the present cheerfully and the future with hope; he must not be forced to devote every thought, all day and every day, to the earning of a livelihood; he must have some leisure to give to the cultivation of his mind and to the enjoyment of the world in which he lives; he must be able to provide himself and those dependent on him with such surroundings as befit a human being; he must not be bowed beneath an overwhelming weight of care for the future of his family—before the best life begins to be possible to him. So long as one of your fellow-citizens, through no fault of his own, is denied the privileges which you yourself possess and which make your life worth living, you, as a good citizen, have something to think about and something to strive for; an injustice to remove, a wrong to right.

CHAPTER XXX.

OUR DEBT TO SOCIETY.

Long ago, a man bought for twenty pounds a piece of land as a spot which is now near the centre of Melbourne. Shortly after, he went away to England, where he lived for the rest of his life; when he died, he left the land, which he had never thought very much about, by will to his son; and the son left it to *his* son. (I do not know that this really happened; but it might have happened.) This last-mentioned person (the grandson of the original buyer) is now an exceedingly wealthy person; for the land which was once worth twenty pounds is now worth hundreds of thousands. To whom does he owe his wealth? Plainly, it is not due to any effort on his own part, nor to any especial industry or foresight on the part of his grandfather. He owes it to the energy and enterprise and hard work of the many thousands of men and women who have caused a great city to grow up where once there was not a single house. He owes his wealth to the collective effort of the community.

Take, again, the case of a man who owned a large tract of land in a country district. (I do know that this really happened. Probably it has often happened.) The farmers of the neighbourhood came to him and asked how much money he would give to help towards putting up a butter factory; but he, not feeling sure that a butter factory would be profitable, would not give a penny. So the farmers went ahead without him, and put up their butter factory, with the result that the district became a prosperous dairying district; and the man who had refused to help was able to sell his land for at least three times what he would have got for it if the factory had not been built. This additional wealth came to him through no effort of his own—for he refused to make any effort; he owed it to the efforts of the community amid which he lived.

Now each of these men may have recognized clearly that he had gained wealth through the work of others; but it is far more likely that each of them thinks of his gaining of wealth as a "stroke of luck," like the picking up of a nugget; it is even possible that they speak of themselves as having "made money," and have got into the habit of regarding themselves as rather clever fellows. And if they speak and think like this, they are just like all the rest of us; for we all constantly forget, or take for granted, innumerable things which we possess and which we would not possess but for the efforts of others, living and dead. We are all apt to forget how poor, and stunted, and bare of all that makes life delightful, our lives would be if it were not for what others have done for us in the past and are doing for us in the present. I need not give many examples; it will be a simple and a very useful exercise for you to go over the things you value most in life and to ask how many of them you have won by your own unaided effort, and for how many you are in *debt to society*.

Take, for instance, language; the language by means of which we have intercourse with our friends—surely one of the chiefest delights of life; the language by means of which we read books, and so enter into communion with the greatest minds the world has known; the language, moreover, in which we think—for no thinking, worth calling thought, is possible to beings that do not possess a language. And if you think the English language a small thing to have inherited, sit down and try to invent a language for yourself; I think a few hours of trying will leave you tired. A language is not invented by one man; it is what we call a *social product*, one

SCHOOL OF MINES AND INDUSTRIES, ADELAIDE.

of the fine fruits of the tree of society. It grows up slowly through the centuries, innumerable men and women contributing to the perfecting of it.

Take, again, the incalculable debt we owe to education; if society did nothing more for us after we left school, we should still be in debt to it till the end of our lives. For education is another social product. Our system of education did not spring up in a single day; it is a fabric that has been slowly raised, like a coral reef, innumerable minds doing their share towards raising it.

I need scarcely remind you of your debt to that small section of society—that little society within the greater—which is called the family; to the love and care and incessant watchfulness by which you were surrounded during the years when you were weak and helpless. Now the family, besides being a society, is itself a social institution. Just as our fathers and mothers have tended us and taught us and guarded us from danger, so does society watch over and protect the family; it is only in the shelter of society that family life is possible.

And when our fathers and mothers can no longer protect us, when we grow up and go out into the world, society does not cease to protect us. It guards our persons and it guards our property. It declares that, however humble and insignificant we may be, no man, however strong and powerful, shall do us any bodily injury or take from us anything that we lawfully possess. We have such a feeling of security that we forget all that society does for us in this respect; we take it for granted—except when we are reading an account of life in some country where life and property are not secure, and where lawlessness rules. Most of all, perhaps, do we take for granted our personal liberty—just because we have been free all our lives, and do not realise what slavery means. We were born free; but we would not have been born free if it had not been for the struggles and labours of others. We sing gaily that "Britons never, never, shall be slaves," and forget that if there had not been countless Britons ready to die for freedom, we might be slaves today. It is not by any strength or skill of our own that we are not serfs to an over-lord or servants to a foreign master.

Among the things for which we are most of all indebted to society are the *moral ideas*—the rules of conduct by which we endeavour to shape our lives—from the humbler virtues, like the "common honesty" which makes commerce possible, and the courtesy which makes social intercourse pleasant, to the highest heights of heroism and nobility. You would be ashamed to tell a lie, to be cowardly in danger, to drink too much, and so forth; but would you, of your own unaided effort, ever have formed the ideas of truthfulness, of courage, of temperance, of justice, of politeness, of endurance, or of any other virtue? No, these ideas were taught you by your father and mother; they were taught you by your school-fellows; you drew them in unconsciously in your childhood, like the air you breathed; they are the moral atmosphere of the society in which you live.

In previous chapters I have spoken of various kinds of public work done by society through the political machine which we call the state. But it is important to realise that it is not only—perhaps not chiefly—by "state action" that society helps us. At every turn we find ourselves helped by the countless generations of the dead; we tread a path worn smooth by multitudes of feet. And at every turn we are helped by our living fellow-citizens. All around us, men are serving us, in ways we take no notice of. Did it ever strike you, how constantly and how carelessly we entrust our lives to others? We step on board a train and allow ourselves to be whirled along with terrific speed without troubling our heads about the danger, because we assume that the lines have been well and truly laid; that the carriages and locomotive have been well and truly made; that the signalmen know their duty and are doing it; and that the driver has learnt his work and is a sober, skilful, and conscientious man. We sleep calmly on ships at sea, a thousand miles from land, because we put implicit trust in the men who are staying awake all night, the men on whose skill and vigilance our safety depends. We call in a doctor when we are sick and obey his orders unquestioningly, because we assume that he has faithfully learnt his business and is faithfully doing his best to serve us. These are obvious instances; but in numberless ways, less obvious, men are serving us well and faithfully. We can never discharge our debt to society; it is too great a debt. But we can at least try to do, in return for all this service, what society asks of us; we can try to be *good citizens*. I must try to show, in another chapter, something of the meaning of this phrase.

CHAPTER XXXI.

OUR DUTY TO SOCIETY

I hope that nothing in the foregoing pages has led you to fancy that "good citizenship" is some special and peculiar kind of goodness; that the "good citizen" is somehow different from the good man or woman. It is not so. The virtues of the good citizen are just the plain, everyday virtues we learn in our own homes. And indeed, the home is the great school and training-ground of citizenship; in our early days, among our brothers and sisters, we may learn all that is needed to fit us for playing our parts in the larger life of the state. For it is in these days that we are taught the great lessons of love and kindness, of obedience and truthfulness, of courtesy and consideration for others, of respect for what is higher and compassion for what is weaker than ourselves; and it is just on these things that good citizenship is based. When we go to school, we find that the same lessons are taught there; there, also, we are trained for the life of the citizen. Along with our arithmetic and geography we learn what is more valuable for us to know than either geography or arithmetic: we learn to do the allotted task to the very best of our ability. But some of the finest lessons given us at school are given out of school hours; in the playground we learn to scorn bullying, sneaking, meanness of all kinds; we learn to respect fair play, and to obey the rules of the game. These schoolboy virtues are the virtues of the grown-up citizen also. Hatred of bullying, love of fair play!—if you come to think of it, just that hatred and just that love have inspired some of the noblest deeds, some of the achievements of which we are proudest, in the history of our race.

Who, then, is the good citizen? Is it the person who obeys the laws of his country—the "law-abiding" person? That will not suffice; obedience to law, while it is certainly a part of good citizenship, is by no means the whole. The laws always lag far behind the conscience of the community; for instance, a man may be an habitual liar without breaking any of the laws of the land. A man may scrupulously obey the law, from fear of the consequences of breaking it, without having a spark of that eager and active spirit of service and sacrifice which makes the good citizen. Again, you sometimes hear people speak as if good citizenship had something to do with voting at parliamentary elections; as if a man were a citizen on the day of choosing representatives in parliament, and merely a private person all the rest of the time. But this is not true; a man cannot put off his citizenship like a garment when the election day is over. To give a careful and well-considered vote is *one* of his duties, but he is a citizen every day, not merely on the days on which he is choosing members of parliament. No: citizenship is a wider thing than that; and if we seek for the essence of it, we shall perhaps find it in that virtue which I have spoken of as being taught us in our homes when we are children: "consideration for others." When a man's desires go out beyond himself, and beyond the little circle of his brothers and sisters and personal friends, to the whole community; when he desires the common good of the community, and desires it so ardently that he is eager to do anything in his power to further it; when he is ready to throw over his own interests when they conflict with the common good; when he is prepared to give up all he possesses, and even life itself, if the welfare of his country demand the sacrifice—that man is, in spirit and truth, a good citizen. And in like manner we may say that the bad citizen is he who uses his country for what he can get out of her, who enriches himself at the expense of the common welfare.

Sometimes we are apt to speak and think as if the welfare of our country had been already secured; as if all the great battles had been fought, and all we require already won for us by the efforts of our fathers. Equality before the law, the right of voting, the right to free speech and free thought, the right to be ruled in accordance with laws made by our own chosen representatives, and so on,—what is there left to struggle for? To speak thus is to mistake the real nature of the civil and political rights which our fathers have handed down to us, and which we rightly hold precious. Precious they are, but as opportunities, not as ends. The telephone is a useful invention; but if, by some peculiarity in the nature of electricity, we were only able to tell each other lies along the wires, we might take small pride in the invention; the value of it depends on the use we can make of it. And so it is with the liberties which have been handed down to us; if we do not know how to use them, they are worth nothing. The voices of those who have walked the earth before us speak in our ears: "Here is liberty, which we won with our blood; it is yours to show that it was worth the winning. Here is the right to vote, which we fought for; it is yours to prove that a vote is worth having. It was ours to struggle for these things; it is yours to use them. And unless you can so use them as to produce by means of them a better and finer country than ours was, then indeed have we worked and fought and died in vain."

A better country! Yes: the good citizen has always before his eyes the fair vision of a country better than his own. Our duty to society is to be discontented with society so long as it harbours one preventable evil. There are some evils which, perhaps, humanity will never be able to prevent; earthquakes, for example. But there is around us a vast mass of evil and suffering which may be prevented by human effort, and so long as this is so, discontent is a duty; and an easy contentment with the present state of things is a vice. All our progress in the past has been due to discontented people; if the contented people had been listened to, we should still be cave-dwellers. It is no part of my task to paint for you *Utopia*, the perfect country; but we need only open our eyes to see how far short of perfection our own country still falls. So long as any injustice is done anywhere in our land, so long as the wealth of the land is unjustly distributed, so long as any man or woman through no fault of their own suffers a degrading poverty, so long as a single child is denied any of the opportunities which ought to be the common birthright of all, there is room for improvement and a field for the active exercise of good citizenship. The good citizen is he who thinks of these things, and who strives with all his might, in however humble a way, to make his country one in which justice prevails, in which freedom is real and no shadow, and in which the spirit of brotherhood rules.

For the spirit of brotherhood is the very essence of society; it is beyond all politics, and it works without any parliament. When an accident in a mine carries off the breadwinners of many families, or when a bush fire sweeps across a district leaving ruin in its track, contributions flow from all parts of the country to the relief of the sufferers; that is a sign that greed and selfishness are not all-powerful, and that human sympathy is awake and active. And this spirit extends sometimes beyond the limits of any one state. When it came to be known, for instance, that the Congo rubber trade was stained by the most horrible atrocities to the natives, indignation was felt all over the civilized world; in England a society was formed for the purpose of putting an end to that evil, and many thousands of pounds were subscribed; some men were even found ready to devote their lives to the cause. Yet those men had very likely never seen a Congo native, and if they did see one they would see little to admire in him, and would have little in common with him. But they felt that they had one thing in common with those savages; they were human beings;

and in the name of our common humanity they vowed to take no rest till that monstrous evil should be put an end to. So, you see, the spirit of brotherhood reaches out from one land to another; and it may be that some day the good citizen will be the citizen of the world; that the human race will be seen as one vast society, suffering together and together striving for the welfare of all; and all men will realise the truth of the words spoken of old, that "we are all members one of another."

And even at present, the citizen's desire must reach out beyond his own country; for he must ardently desire that his own country may act rightly in its relations with other countries. There are times, alas! in the history of every land, when good men must needs be ashamed of their country. As we read the history of Britain, for instance, it is impossible not to see that there are pages in it of which we cannot be proud. But we may take comfort in remembering that in Britain's worst hours she has never lacked loyal sons to protest against the errors of the majority; men who, knowing that the worst calamity which can befall a nation is to fall from righteousness, have striven with all their might to make their countrymen see the right course and pursue it. And the man who can do that, however unpopular he may make himself at the time, comes to be known in the long run for the very best kind of citizen.

But for the most part, the citizen's chief concern is with the community of which he is himself a member. To make the society in which we live a true *Commonwealth*, in the best sense of the term—not a mere collection of persons scrambling for wealth, each one seeking his own selfish ends without regard for others,—but a hearty comradeship for all noble purposes, each one striving for the good of all, and all together seeking for the most splendid and beautiful life possible to human beings,—that is the task of citizenship.

APPENDIX: PREFERENTIAL VOTING

In several of the Australian States, the plan known as "preferential voting" has been adopted for general elections. This is not quite so simple as the old system, but it is far more fair; and it is not too complicated to be understood by anyone who will spend a few minutes on the effort to understand it.

We shall suppose that you are a voter in a constituency in which 1,000 persons vote, and which returns one member to Parliament. There are three candidates, whom we shall call Pitt, Peel, and Gladstone. Under the old system you could only say "I want Pitt"—or Peel, or Gladstone, as the case may be. The preferential system allows you to say "I want Pitt, but if I cannot have Pitt I should prefer Peel to Gladstone;" and that preference is taken into account.

The old system might give this result: Gladstone, 340; Peel, 335; Pitt, 325; Gladstone would be declared elected. He would be elected although, out of 1,000 voters, 660 had voted against him, and only 340 for him. In such a case the wishes of the great majority of the voters would be entirely disregarded. The preferential system is an attempt to make the wishes of the majority prevail.

By the preferential system, you do not simply put a mark opposite Gladstone's name on your voting paper if you wish Gladstone elected; you have to show whether you would prefer Peel or Pitt if you cannot have Gladstone. You do this by means of numerals:

3. Pitt.

1. Gladstone.

2. Peel.

You have given Gladstone what is called your "first preference," and Peel your "second preference,"—which means that you would rather have Peel than Pitt.

When the votes are first counted, only the "first preferences" are taken any notice of. This is called the "first count," and it might result as follows:

Gladstone,	340.
Peel,	335.
Pitt,	325.

If Gladstone had received 501 votes (that is, if he had been put first on the list by more than half of the thousand voters,) the election would be over; but as he has only received 340 votes, a "second count" is necessary.

Since Pitt received the smallest number of first preferences, his chance of being elected is gone. The papers of the 325 who gave Pitt their first preference are now examined again, in order to find out to whom they gave their second preference. It is found that 200 of them gave their second preference to Peel, and 125 to Gladstone. These are added to the votes received by Peel and Gladstone respectively on the "first count"; and the result is—

Gladstone,	465.
Peel,	535.

Peel is therefore declared to have won the election.

INDEX